The Hyperion Library of World Literature

CLASSICS OF RUSSIAN LITERATURE

ALEKSEI REMIZOV

The Clock

AUTHORIZED TRANSLATION

BY

JOHN COURNOS

HYPERION PRESS, INC.

Westport, Connecticut

Published in 1924 by Chatto & Windus, London
Hyperion reprint edition 1977
Library of Congress Catalog Number 76-23894
ISBN 0-88355-509-3 (cloth ed.)
ISBN 0-88355-510-7 (paper ed.)
Printed in the United States of America

Library of Congress Cataloging in Publication Data

Remizov, Aleksei Mikhailovich, 1877-1957.
  The clock.

  (The Hyperion library of world literature) (Classics of Russian literature)
  Reprint of the 1924 ed. published by Chatto and Windus, London.
  CONTENTS: The clock. — A white heart. — The betrothed. — Easter.
  I. Title.
PZ3.R2849Cl 12   [PG3470.R4]   891.7'3'44   76-23894
ISBN 0-88355-509-3
ISBN 0-88355-510-7 pbk.

Contents

*

FOREWORD

ALEKSEI REMIZOV, author of mystery plays and fairy-tales, of short stories and novels, which fill more than a dozen volumes, occupies a conspicuous position among living Russian writers. In the Dostoevsky tradition, which is the greatest of all forces shaping contemporary Russian literature, Remizov differs from the author of *Crime and Punishment* chiefly in that he is more conscious of his style ; no writer has such an immense vocabulary, especially of root words, to which he has striven to give orchestral values. These factors render his work difficult of translation ; much of his work is, indeed, untranslatable, though in the original extremely beautiful and suggestive as word music : his words, even when obscure to Russians themselves, have a peculiar living quality. Nothing could be simpler, however, than his simple compositions, and *The Clock*, *A White Heart*, and the two prose poems included in this volume may be counted as such. *The Betrothed* is an especially charming example in the way of a prose-ballad, a form in which he has shown himself a master, and by which he has re-created numerous Russian legends and folk-tales. In this particular one he has given new life to the old legend of the Snowdrop.

FOREWORD

The tendency to pity is strong in this author. In this he is essentially Russian and related to Dostoevsky, whom he also resembles in the presentation of dual types, demonic as well as godly. Love of Russia flames through all his work, so that it is not astonishing to see him sometimes digress into prophecy ; how true, one may gather from a little tale, *The Saviour's Flame*, written as far back as 1913. It begins with the phrase, " There's no God in St. Petersburg ! " and concludes with a description of the Passion night in St. Petersburg, before the Kazan Cathedral, after the services : " The entire square trembled with little flames ; gravely quiet, the people issued from the church, distributed among the houses the Saviour's holy flame . . . Russia is aflame ! yonder in the starry space, there poured out across the broad Russian earth, in a flaming Volga, the dinning, terrible glow ; Russia is aflame ! The Saviour's Passion flame shall preserve her, the Russian people shall not perish. And if it has been already determined and appointed by God that we must accept destruction, that Russia must perish, then the Russian people shall go even to its death with the little flame, and the Passion flame will take it there, the little flame will preserve its soul. And though we are broken, though we are jeered at, though we are lost, the Saviour's Passion flame shall preserve the soul, the dear name of Russia."

FOREWORD

As I re-read this passage, I am reminded of
its author, whom I had the pleasure of meeting
in Petrograd during the first months of the Bol-
shevik Revolution. I remember him as a man
of about forty, a strange little figure, somewhat
bowed ; with high, broad forehead, a face charac-
teristically Russian ; it somehow gave me the
impression of belonging to a benign demon ! In
straitened circumstances, like all the writers of
the time, he worked in a small room, hardly wider
than an ordinary house corridor. The lower
part of the window, the greater half, was draped
in black, so that the miserable winter light stole
in from the top as in a studio. Several old ikons,
on which he is an authority, were ranged in front
of him on his writing-table. High, slender tapers
burned before the holy images ; that was one
"luxury," of which he could not deprive himself.
"How do you manage to live ?" I asked him,
being aware of the material conditions to which
even the most successful writers had fallen.
"Like a bird in the fields ! " was his reply, which
is not as cryptic as it sounds. For we know
that his contemporary, Alexander Blok, died soon
after, according to all accounts from under-
nourishment. Luckily, Remizov has lately managed to escape from Russia, and it is to be hoped
that he will, in some future narrative, tell us
something about life in Russia during these
unhappy years. And if *A White Heart*, an episode

FOREWORD

of the Revolution, is a thing to judge by, I feel sure that it will not be a bitter, but a pitying thing !

J. C.

EAST PRESTON,
    SUSSEX.

NOTE

OF the shorter sketches in this volume, *A White Heart* was published in THE DIAL, *The Betrothed* in THE EGOIST, and *Easter* in THE WESTMINSTER GAZETTE. The translator wishes to express his indebtedness in each case.

The Clock

PART ONE
Chapter I

KOSTYA KLOTCHKOV was the boy in the clock-shop kept by the Klotchkovs. Kostya had just gone out to wind up the clock in the cathedral belfry ; one evening each week, Kostya wound up the clock in the cathedral belfry, and every evening he had to see that it was in working order.

" Kostya, why is your nose crooked ? " came the cry, borne, as it were, upon the wind, and struck his ear.

In his rage Kostya bit his long, pitiful lower lip and winced : it was quite true, his nose was crooked.

No matter how much Kostya shrunk within himself, how much he tried to hide, he fell foul of people's eyes ; his hood did not protect him ; the wind kept on tearing it off. And the passers-by let no chance slip to annoy the deformed boy and to laugh at him.

Such were the passers-by. Such was Kostya.

Kostya was pushing his way through the crowded streets towards the cathedral, to wind up the clock in the cathedral belfry.

The clock's keys rattled in Kostya's pocket. With these terrible keys he might have fractured

3

the most stubborn skull in that crowd of provoking pedestrians, but his accursed stigma—the nose which stuck out sidewise—gave him no rest. The accursed stigma spread like a wound, as if it were not on his face but somewhere in his heart, and its burden grew heavier from day to day, became more and more an encumbrance, and gave a stoop to his back.

And he would lose heart.

More than once, at home, Kostya stood before the mirror and pressed his fingers against his crooked nose. He wanted his nose to be as correctly shaped as *in a picture*! And he pressed his fingers against his nose until it appeared to him to have become perfectly straight.

But this only appeared to him; everything was as before, and worse. Kostya used to be caught before the mirror, which provoked laughter; not infrequently he fell into a rage, threw himself at his tormentors and bit them. He always caught something for that!

And he would lose heart.

" If only to-morrow, to-morrow morning, when I open my eyes, and go to the mirror, and suddenly find myself different. Then all will say : ' Kostya ! ' " Kostya, growing thoughtful, clicked his tongue with pleasure. " ' Kostya,' they will say, ' your nose ' . . ."

" Kostya, why is your nose crooked ? " again

4

came the cry, borne, as it were, upon the wind, and struck his ear.

"It's a lie! It's a lie!" Kostya shouted down the street at the top of his voice.

But how could he defend himself against importunate pursuit, how could he outshout this accursed hammering cry that pursued him even in the whistling of the wind?

He felt short of breath; a cold blast struck his body.

Kostya recalled the insults, the taunts and the nicknames which it had been his lot to hear in the course of his brief, deformed existence, and those which he himself had thought of in his irritation. They fell about his head; they appeared to pinch him behind his hood, to creep under the collar of his shirt and to bite into his chest. And having bit through his chest they flowed together into a vile leech. And this leech began to suck at Kostya's heart.

Well, he would open his eyes on the morrow, walk up to the mirror, and what then? What sort of eyes had he? One asquint, the other bulging. Asquint and bulging. Not really eyes, but eyesores. And no one would ever fit him with either new nose or new eyes—never! As he was born, so he would die—a fool and a simpleton. If not a fool and a simpleton, then an idiot—there was not much to choose between these.

THE CLOCK

His hands, stuck deep in his pocket, burned ; his fingers smarted with the frost.

Such vermin attaches itself to a being, such a leech, and then watch out ! It will have no pity, it will exhaust one ; suck one's heart out.

Suddenly Kostya began to cry, and through his tears he saw himself a silly fool ; after all, that was what they called him, a fool, a simpleton, an idiot ; he did not walk like others, but somehow sidewise ; he did not laugh like others, but somehow with a sudden outburst ; he did everything in an odd, unhuman way.

But how should he act ? Who would teach him ?

Why not put an end to himself ? Or had he not the courage to make up his mind ? If he had not, then besides being a fool, a simpleton, and an idiot, he was also a thorough good-for-nothing. A whimpering beggar. Well, why did he go on living ? Day after day he stuck in the shop, evenings he went to the belfry to see to the clock. What was the good of his seeing to the clock ? That it should go on, not stop ? That it should go on evenly and tediously from hour to hour ? And here they were pinching him, and would go on pinching him. He had a crooked nose ! But the trouble did not lie in the clock or the nose. In general, what was the use of life ?

Kostya stopped short. Through his tears his

6

trembling lips hummed a nursery song, a song he had heard Khristina, the wife of his brother Sergey, sing over her Irinushka. And it seemed to him as he hummed this tune that he was speaking with some one, that some one was casting a ray of light on his dark, deformed life. It seemed to him as if all his bitterness were becoming lost in this barely audible song : that no one would hear what struggled within him, that no one would see what ached within him ; and that which grieved within him would never become revealed, and that which was dying within him would die once and for all. But he wished to live. Oh, how he would live if it were only possible that to-morrow, on waking, he could see himself in the mirror another being, with another nose, a nose as in a picture !

Kostya stood there, stretched himself full length, and burnt like a candle.

A lump of snow flew past Kostya, but Kostya did not notice it ; then a second lump struck him violently, as if with a strong wing, but Kostya did not notice that either ; a third lump, like a bird, struck the top of his head, and Kostya lurched forward, his nose on the cold, wind-swept pavement, and everything suddenly became extinguished.

Kostya, small and altogether strange, lay flat, not daring to move. He felt as if a stone were upon him, as if a stone had grown cold before his eyes. It was as if everything had died, and no other life left round him in the world. No, everything remained alive, only he had died. Kostya had died !

Having evoked this picture of sudden death, Kostya grew terrified : as he wanted to live. Oh, how he would live if it were only possible that to-morrow, on waking, he could see himself in the mirror another being, with another nose, with a nose as in a picture !

And blow after blow, as of heavy clock-weights, came down on his back, thumped him between the shoulders : it was some boys who had way-laid Kostya and made an onslaught upon him with snowballs.

Shrieking with pain, Kostya briskly got on his feet and began to run.

He ran like a dog with a maimed leg, and yelped like a dog.

" What do you mean bumping into people ? " snarled passers-by.

" One would think the devil was after you ! "

" Get out of the way, you devil-face," shouted the cabbies.

The evening, growing darker, swathed the earth in a shroud, joined and merged houses and factory chimneys, lit the lunar flame, and lifted up the moon.

Kostya touched his nose with his crushed, sticky fingers, which felt so large that they did not appear to be his own : blood flowed from his nose, smeared his lips, and thickened in his throat.

"Oh, you son of a dog, I'll——" suddenly turned Kostya, and with all his might struck out his fist into the iron lamp-post.

Then he realized with sudden clearness that he, Kostya Klotchkov, crooked-nosed Kostya, was a being in himself, and that everything round him was quite another thing, and that he could overturn this other thing—the whole world. He could overturn the whole world, and he knew how to do it.

Kostya strode on with a firm step, feeling no longer either pain or kicks or blows ; he boldly thrust out his crooked-nosed face and made a defiant gesture with his crooked nose.

Only his heart, like a lump of ice, floated in his hot breast. While in his pocket the keys of the clock rattled.

Kostya clutched hold of his keys, and as he renewed faith in himself and his resolution, ready to move mountains, he became transformed, as it were, into a key ; and as a key he drifted confidently along in a kind of a drunken half-dream.

Kostya traversed street after street, lane after lane, made his way through snowdrifts, glided across icy places, confidently, in a kind of a drunken half-dream.

THE CLOCK

At first hardly more than a glimmer, each step brought nearer, larger and whiter, the stone cathedral belfry with its golden dome under the stars.

Chapter II

KOSTYA did not count the steps in the belfry, but there appeared to be more of them than usual, one steeper than the other. He lodged his foot high, but his hold gave way.

At every step he met with the wind. The wind shook him, deafened him, tugged at his hood with its long frosty fingers, and assailed his eyes with its icy nippers. And the hoary bells gave out sounds of wailing.

Kostya glanced at the bells and climbed higher. By the time he got to the top of the belfry he could barely breathe.

But there was no time for dallying. Kostya got to work : having raised himself on his tiptoes, and bit his drooping lip, he caught hold of the huge winding lever with his numbed hands, and, straining his whole chest forward, he began to turn.

Awakened suddenly, as it were, grown younger, the clock began to hiss and to groan, to give forth sounds as from an old chilled throat. Then it grew silent. No, it was ticking—with a heavy movement, swinging slowly from side to side, giving itself up to God's will, for it saw no end : it had no end ; it had neither strength nor will to stop once and for all its appointed course.

THE CLOCK

The cold, benumbed Kostya suddenly grew warmer.

His mouth slightly open, his half-battered teeth clenched tightly, Kostya caught hold of an iron rod, and pushing it forward as if it were no more than a feather, he swung towards the window opening, clambered deftly on to the sill, bent himself in two, and reaching out his hand in a super-human way, he touched the big hand of the clock with the trembling rod, hooked it and led it forward, until it pointed a full hour ahead on the dial.

The minutes sped in the wake of the hand, unable to pause, unable to sing their minute song, and they ran on in the circle—forward—from quarter-past to half-past, from half-past to a quarter to, then to ten minutes to, then from ten to to five to, from five to to four to . . .

Kostya drew back the iron rod, releasing the clock hand, and in the terrible height, swept by a rude, unfriendly wind, waited for the clock to strike. Then stretching his neck forward in goose-like fashion, and resting his bony hands on the stone window-sill, he looked below on the swarming town which he had duped. He could not longer repress the ebullient feeling of his boundless power, he could not shut his lips, which were distorted with laughter.

Tears sprang from his laughter, and the tears were shattered by this sobbing laughter.

THE CLOCK

The obedient clock hand, completing the circle, was approaching its last point.

Then the clock bell swung its cast-iron tongue in its singing heart and began to sing its ancient, immutable song ; the bell struck its hour.

The clock could not stay its appointed strokes. Ten strokes rolled by, one after another : nine appointed by God, the tenth by Kostya.

Terror and wailing and laughter tore themselves from the singing heart of the bell.

The moon, dimmed by a frosty cloud, glided, naked, across the sky, and the dying tones of the bell, rising from the earth, crept upward, like a mist, and covered the moon's body as with a veil.

And everything upon the earth grew painfully quiet.

Suddenly a wild outcry pierced the painful stillness. Kostya was singing. Kostya Klotchkov, who knew how to overturn the world ; the all-powerful Kostya, who held *Time* itself in his hand.

As he finished his proud song, Kostya spat below on the swarming town which he had duped.

The town, which lived according to the cathedral clock, gave a start.

A fireman in the watch-tower, wrapped in his sheepskin, his terrible bronze helmet on his head, suddenly paused and began to look for the fire, but the red glow above the belfry died out, and the fireman once more began to pace round the four dark signal balls and ringing wires. The departing trains, an hour late, speeded up under increased steam, and whistled desperately. Hungry, jaded horses were lashed on by the cabbies, themselves under the whip of nervous, belated passengers hurrying to keep their appointments. A telegraph operator, bent into a harness arch, made his exhausted finger dance even more briskly across the keys of his instrument : breaking off messages and sending across all sorts of nonsense and cock-and-bull stories. Young *ladies* from the gay " New World " were roused from their unfinished sleep, and, in expectation of guests, smeared white paint across their spotted blue cheeks and the ineradicable ulcers upon their worn, crumpled breasts. The notary, glad of the hour, and finishing the day's business, was putting into his portfolio a pile of lapsed bills for protest. The graveyard watchman, a spade under his arm, was on his way to dig graves for to-morrow's corpses. The publican was opening up his last bottles. And the government dram-shop was being closed. Misery and sorrow and all their sisters passed through the town gate, scattered themselves throughout the town, entered the houses of the fated ones. And the marked soul was agitated. As he looked with his senseless eyes upon the dimmed full moon, tipsy in a cloud of mist, the crazed Markusha-

THE CLOCK

Napoleon delightedly uttered his night prayer :
" O Lord, cast upon us Thy light of the sun,
the moon and the stars ! "

Slowly and deliberately Kostya descended from
the belfry, then locked it and limped his way
home.

There was no fear in his soul, no pain, but
only spurts of unappeasable laughter :

" I changed it to ten o'clock, and it struck
ten, ho, ho ! If I like I can make it midnight—
I'll defy the devil, ho, ho ! I'll go home now
and have some tea. I like tea best of all."

For a short while Kostya plunged into that
darkness and oblivion from which not a single
voice comes. His heart brimmed over with
pride.

Chapter III

KOSTYA'S small hunched figure, looking in its hood very much like a hare, hopped peacefully along the river, and darted out of the snowdrifts.

Kostya paused before the Governor's house, lingered there as he glanced through the gates; then went on his way.

What was in Kostya's mind? What did he want? His oblivious mood was slowly dispersing; his thoughts roused him with vague voices, held him and released him. He went on because some one drove him on; he swerved to aside because some one led him there; he halted because some one's hand held him back.

The house porters were shutting the gates for the night. Evil dogs were being let loose in the yards. Homeless nocturnal people were already beginning to appear in the streets; they stealthily hid themselves here and there, lurked near walls, and within wall gates; the cold kept them shivering and on the jump.

"I'll go in and have a look at my charmer," thought Kostya suddenly, and increased his pace. And now he strode on, immersed in a single, undivided thought: He would *go in and have a look at his charmer.*

Once near the Lisitsins' trinket-shop, he looked

in through the window and, snorting with pleasure, flew into the shop like a snowball.

"Good evening, how are you?" Kostya stretched out his hand and seized Lydotchka's little one.

Lydotchka, the daughter of the proprietor, made a grimace with her sugary, porcelain little nose, and said not a word.

"Well, Kostya, is it hot?" said the shop assistant, a fellow with sandy hair, white eyelashes, and a bald-growing pate; nicknamed *Wise Little Head*.

"Go out and see for yourself whether it's hot!" said Kostya boldly as he looked rather loftily at Wise Little Head.

"I am thinking," persisted the shop assistant, "that your little nose has been exposed too much to the sun."

"And your hair is falling out, Wise Little Head!"

The irritated shop assistant said with a nasty snigger:

"You'd better go and take a stroll, Kostya; we've missed you horribly!"

Kostya, refusing the rebuff, mumbled something under his nose and lingered near the counter.

The frowning shop assistant was wrapping up boxes, Lydotchka was counting the cash.

"Good night!" Kostya with a flourish unbuttoned his overcoat, and, slamming the door, walked out from the Lisitsins' shop, reeling like a drunkard. Without again buttoning up his overcoat, he crossed the street, to his own shop.

The Klotchkov shop was being closed.

Through the window grating could be seen a tin, shadeless lamp which sleeplessly watched through the night. The lamp stood under the gaping metal mouth of a huge gramophone, stilled as it were in a moment of yawning. The clocks were ticking all around upon the walls ; there were such different ones and such odd ones : some, as if they were undergoing convulsions ; others with a sour smile ; and still others which had hurt, bitter, or mocking expressions. And all possible gold trifles and gew-gaws grew dim in their oblivion : some content that they had not fallen into the hands of a buyer ; others, on the other hand, enraged because no one bought them ; still others indifferent, and self-satisfied, and winking shrewdly. The objects were permeated with a kind of unsightliness and tedium, which reminded one of the inevitable end that comes to every one in his hour, without asking.

Outside, the street was in a bustle.

Shutters were being put on doors, locks were being put on cross-bars, there was a rattling of keys.

There was quite a gathering in the shop. There was the master goldsmith, Semyon Mitrofanovitch, a bloated man with small, colourless eyes, a creature all withered and flabby, rather broad-looking because of the fur overcoat thrown loosely over his shoulders with sleeves dangling; and Motya—brother of the shop's mistress, Khristina Mikhailovna—a slightly deaf shop assistant with thin, droll moustaches; and Raya —Kostya's elder sister—a pale, active girl; and Ivan Trofimitch, a young boy with a grave, unchildlike face which gave not the slightest hint of his height, and appeared crushed under a worn fur cap; and the mistress of the house herself, the first beauty in town, Khristina Mik-hailovna Klotchkov; and the flap-eared dog Koupon. Only the master of the house was not there—Sergey Andreyevitch Klotchkov.

"Allow me to ask," said the master goldsmith as the mistress was about to leave the room, "will Sergey Andreyevitch be here to-morrow?"

"What do you want?" Khristina glanced at him, measured him with her eyes, and, turning sharply, walked out.

Kostya, who annoyed every one and was driven away by every one, burst into a cackle, and, catching the master goldsmith by an empty sleeve, and choking and interrupting himself as he talked, began to tell about his meeting with Lydotchka Lisitsina, and how he had got the best of Wise Little Head, and how Lydotchka made eyes at him.

"If only your brother, Sergey Andreyevitch ——" interrupted the master goldsmith.

" What lovely eyes has Lydotchka ! "

" That's how things happen nowadays. People think of going up the flue, and so they've no wish to pay up. They're not people, they are bounders."

" Do you know, Semyon Mitrofanovitch, I have an interesting peculiarity ; when I come in I shake people's hands, when I go out I don't."

" Your brother, to be sure, has taken to his heels ; but he'll be caught, mind you, and he'll have to sit out his time in solitary confinement," went on the master goldsmith.

" Why in solitary ? "

" It's all very simple. He's gone up the flue ; ruined, in fact, bankrupt. That's one thing. Then again, he hasn't paid his bills, and has made illegal concealments. Well, they'll catch the good fellow and put him in jail ; he'll have his chance to lick the tails of rats and count black-beetles."

" Count black-beetles ? " repeated Kostya after him, and in his agitation let go the master gold-smith's sleeve, and rushed out at full speed after Khristina.

He ran like one possessed, but Khristina was far ahead ; she glided along the street without a pause. He fell violently against a kerbstone, but though in pain he picked himself up again and made another spurt at full speed.

THE CLOCK

"Khristina! Khristina! Khristina!" Kostya
cried at the top of his voice.

Khristina looked round at last.

"Where is Seryozha?" shouted Kostya.

There was no answer.

"Where is Seryozha?" cried Kostya in a rage.

"It's none of your business, idiot; shut up!"
Khristina cut him short.

Kostya, irritated, began to sniff. He spite-
fully paced behind, and held the distraught
Khristina as if on a cord, which entwined itself
around her heart and tightened at every step;
she was powerless to free herself.

"It's a hard life," muttered Kostya. "I lie
down and I can't sleep, the *zalezniak** is worry-
ing my inside."

"That's what comes of running about with all
your clothes unbuttoned, and you oughtn't to
read either. D'you understand?"

"I talk to myself, and everything wakens me.
Which is more correct: wakens or awakens?"

"You'll come to a bad end!" Khristina had
but one thought: when would this idiot leave
her in peace? He was so repugnant to her.

"Guess whom I've seen to-day?"

Khristina shrugged her shoulders.

"Mr. Nelidov!" exclaimed Kostya. "I went

* *Zalezniak*—literally, the "creeper-in"; the word suggests
a worm-like object by its likeness in construction to *tcherviak*
(worm).

21

to the chemist's to get some face ointment, and there was Nelidov—at the chemist's."

Khristina paused on hearing Nelidov's name. She recalled her husband's friend, and she wanted to see him at once : he was the only man who might do something to save them.

" A great misfortune has happened, he said," continued Kostya.

" What ? "

" A great misfortune has happened, he said. . . . But where is Seryozha ? "

Khristina made a sudden spurt forward, and, without looking round, went on quickly, all the time faster and faster.

" Ho-ho ! " Kostya let fly after her.

Kostya walked with an important air. He suddenly felt happy because he had frightened Khristina, and he marvelled at his own powers. And if he chose, they would all be afraid of him ; they would come to him and implore him for mercy, and he would put them all in solitary confinement ; they would lick the tails of rats and count black-beetles. He took the keys from his pocket, and, holding them in one of his hands like a sceptre, now bowed, now smiled at some one ; he, Kostya Klotchkov, would rule over Time itself.

In this manner Kostya reached the house. He climbed the fence and got into a small garden, and stealthily made his way to the window.

THE CLOCK

At the table by the window sat his young sister Katya, with frowning forehead, over her lessons.

Kostya suddenly thought of a trick : he knocked on the window and hid himself. Katya grew nervous. Then he approached the window again, and, making a horrible face, pressed it against the pane. Katya jumped up in fright and waved her arms.

"Ho-ho !" snorted Kostya, and proudly walked into the house.

Yes, if Kostya chose, they would all be afraid of him. They would come to him and implore him for mercy, and he would put them all in solitary confinement ; they would lick the tails of rats and count black-beetles.

Chapter IV

FROSYA, the Klotchkovs' housemaid, all tucked up, with puffed-up hair like Raya's, was struggling to get away from Kostya.

But Kostya had no intention of letting Frosya go ; showing his teeth, he tightened his hold on Frosya and clove to her like a little beast.

"Get away, you nosy idiot ; can't you let me alone !" Frosya pulled about with her arms, pinched "the unbearable leech," and, finally, she swung one of her arms back and struck Kostya a stinging blow on his mouth, felling him to the floor.

It was not the first time this happened. Kostya picked himself up, put himself in order, and dreadfully sniffing, went upstairs into the dining-room.

"Wretch, miserable wretch !" sniffed Kostya.

Khristina sat alone in the dining-room before the samovar. Still hot, the samovar was flickering out : something moved within it and knocked ; it was like the knocking of the train at night when you cannot sleep.

Khristina silently put a cup of tea and a lump of bread before Kostya.

Kostya sipped a mouthful, then stuffed his mouth with bread until his cheeks swelled out ; he went on eating greedily, mincing and munching his food.

THE CLOCK

But Khristina did not appear to hear his eating music; she was locked in a tight circle, from which she was no longer able to extricate herself.

That same day her husband Sergey—Sergey Andreyevitch Klotchkov—had left town; he had no choice but to leave; there was no place for him here, and nothing to do: the Klotchkovian affairs had taken a turn for the worse; there was nothing to pay bills with, and no one to tide them over. And so he had left town, and would not return until he had found means to improve his ruined business.

Wholly possessed by this one thought, that Sergey would not return, perhaps never return, Khristina recalled step by step everything that had happened during the day, from the instant that the inevitable stood up face to face with her and closed every path and destroyed the last loop-hole of escape—the faith that something would happen to restore everything to its old state; in short, her faith in a miracle.

She pursued Sergey in her thoughts. She recalled their farewell, the ring of the third bell, the departure of the train. And, having evoked the whole scene from the first to the last moment, she suddenly remembered one solemn Te Deum on the departure of soldiers for the war, when at the moment the priest recited a prayer for the warriors—for those who were going, for those who were fighting, and for those who were imprisoned—a reserve-man jumped out of the ranks, seized an infant from the arms of his wife and suffocated it. And, in remembering that solemn Te Deum, she shook her head.

One and the same thought went on turning in her head : it was that Sergey would not return, perhaps never return.

She pursued Sergey in her thoughts. She had just overtaken the train. She is in the same carriage with him, at his side ; but he does not see her ; yes, he does see her, but he dare not raise his eyes. This inevitability, which closed every path and destroyed the last loop-hole of escape—the faith that something would happen to restore everything to its old state, the faith in a miracle—this inevitability prevented him from lifting his eyes. And once more, having evoked the whole scene from the first to the last moment, she let her thoughts jump to the morning of that same day, when she and he sat together here in the dining-room, and everything appeared to have come to an end, and there was no faith left in any sort of miracle.

And having thought of that last morning, she shook her head.

But how did she come to forget Nelidov ? He was Sergey's companion and friend, and he might have saved them ! And Nelidov was such a man ; he would have found the means, he would have saved them !

And one and the same thought kept turning in her mind, that already it was too late, that Nelidov could not help them, and that Sergey would not return, perhaps never return.

She pictured clearly to herself: the sleepy carriage in which Sergey was travelling. Sergey was not asleep, but had lost himself for a moment; then suddenly something prodded him, his heart trembled. Why should he not return? She watched him rise, look out of the window, but the train ran on—it could hardly be expected to take heed of him; and wherever he looked he saw the white fields—these also showed no concern. Who, then, would? But there must be some one, some one to show some concern! And he did not know what to do. The train ran on, the carriage was asleep, the white fields were asleep.

"Ha!" Kostya choked on his tea and sneezed into his cup.

Khristina gave a start as if awakened, and an altogether unexpected thought struck her with great suddenness: "They were brothers by blood, these two, Sergey and Kostya!" And, having recalled how for an instant that evening she had mistaken Kostya for Sergey, she could not forgive herself this self-deception and went on thinking: "Even their ears are alike, and also . . ." And as she thought, she frowned squeamishly.

Just then the circle of those other inevitable thoughts, as if taking vengeance for that moment of reflection, sharply locked itself in. How she would have liked just then to jump up and set up a cry through the whole house, run out in the street and cry up and down the street, take a stand in the square and make the whole town, the whole world, hear her ; and in her cry to kill her sadness, her indignation, and her despair : for she did not know why all this had come upon her and why she had to suffer.

In answer, like a taunt, sounds of a choking cough suddenly filled the room, grew in volume, now broke into sharp explosive chortles, not into a prolonged snore, and again burst into a kind of staccato of choking sound.

It was as if some one, out of spite, were scraping glass with a blunt knife under her very ears. And there was no way to shut out the noise, and no place where she could escape it.

All huddled in his greasy, brown dressing-gown, and shuffling with his slippers, a hunched, feeble old man came creeping up slowly to the table ; it was the father Klotchkov, Andrey Petrovitch. Silently, with a trembling hand, the old man pulled up a chair. But he had barely seated himself and secured a seeming respite than he was seized with pain ; he feverishly threw open his dressing-gown, and convulsively clutched with his bony fingers at his hairy breast

28

and emitted a snore-like sound. And for a long time something irrepressible seethed in his hairy breast, and no human power could stop this seething.

"Has Seryozha left?" asked the old man as he caught his breath.

"You know yourself," answered Khristina Feodorovna dryly, without glancing at the old man, while she cursed him in her heart.

"Yes, he's a liar, a hypocrite, and a rake," she abused the old man in her heart. "Yes, he's lying, dissembling, wants to be let alone, not bothered or asked for help, and he has money"—she knew that!—"but he doesn't want to part with his money, doesn't want to save his son from misfortune—the accursed liar, hypocrite, and rake!"

And as she cursed him, she clutched at all those indignities, all those reproaches, which in moments of spite, provocation, and despair are born in the heart of one human being against another.

The old man appeared to her half naked, filthy, wasted away by senile disease ; she saw his toothless slavery mouth, his dull, bulging eyes, his trembling hands. . . . Niusha, the cook, with her sleeves rolled up, was rubbing his breast, and he moved his hands upon her hands, and, helpless, was sniffing audibly, like Kostya. Then those eternal mustard poultices, which touched one's heart somewhere with a burn.

"Ugh! You've poisoned your wife, accursed, wretched old man; you've poisoned all your children, and you've brought this idiot into the world, and you yourself are like a dog in a manger!" Her hate and rancour blazed out: for he had money and would not save them.

Whether it was that the old man had overheard his daughter-in-law's secret thoughts, or that such a long while had passed, he blinked guiltily with his eyes, and, evidently having lost all hope of anyone handing him the bread, he stretched out his hand toward the biscuit-box, but in spite of all efforts could not reach it.

Kostya saw this, and he crawled across the whole table, pulling the table-cloth after him, and upsetting a glass of tea with his sleeve. The glass rolled over and struck the floor in much the same way that Kostya struck the floor under Frosya's fist.

Khristina threw up her arms, gave a strange look, and, flinging down her keys, walked out of the room.

"Again I've made a mess of it," grumbled Kostya, wiping the tea from his clothes. "Oh, well!"

When his daughter-in-law's footsteps died away, the old man closed his eyes; then, after another minute had lapsed, he slowly rose from his chair, and, glancing timidly round, stuck a full five fingers into the box of chocolates. Having helped himself to a handful, he began to pick the chocolates off his palm and to gulp them down greedily without pause, very much as a hungry bird would gulp. Long since, the old man took it into his head that he was a kind of gulping-machine ; that he could consume as many sweets as he could cram into himself. Besides, he had to make up for lost time ! he hadn't gratified his taste for sweets a long while !

Having eaten to his heart's content, until he could hold no more, the old man resumed his hunch, and, sipping his nasty, insipid, flavourless tea, reflected bitterly upon his old age and dog's life.

He had given the shop to his son Sergey, and he had given a great deal of money to set him up—all squandered ! How much labour he had given to it, how many privations he had undergone ; he had scraped together farthings, underslept nights, bent his back ; denied himself everything—all squandered ! As for gratitude, they were treating him like a dog—yes, like a dog ! Now they wanted him to give them money. What money ? He had no money ! In all conscience, in all truth, he had not a battered farthing to his soul. Even if he had money, he would not have given Sergey another penny. What was the use of giving Sergey money ? To let it blow away in the wind ? No, that's nonsense ! Money is not given for to be blown away in the wind ; money is for to keep a business going. It is true he might have got a little for Sergey, just enough to save Sergey ; but he did not want to, he did not want to because they were treating him like a dog—yes, like a dog ; they wanted to drive him into his grave, as if he hadn't one foot in it already !

" I can and I don't want to. I might manage to get hold of some money, but I shan't ! " the old man went on repeating to himself, and this thought about his own powers warmed his old body wasted by senile disease.

" Kostya," the old man called affectionately, " have you read to-day's paper ? "

" I don't read papers, papa. I'm not that kind of a person ! " Kostya was picking off the petals of a flower that bloomed that morning, thinking that the flower thereby gained in splendour.

" Oh, you philosopher ! " said the old man with a wink.

" Animals, papa," said Kostya as he went on tearing off the petals, " lawyers' speeches, wild savages ; in general, anything philosophical, that is my passion, because nature is truly all. . . . Travels, the germination of a million different creatures, how they come into existence, what their purpose and significance are—that is food for me. That's the sort of thing I want to read.

THE CLOCK

But the war does not interest me ; it's a sport for small children."

"Kostya, you are stupid, you talk nonsense, gnats and flies will eat you up !" The old man reached across for the sardines, and, pulling out fish by fish with his fingers, he ate them greedily.

"Papa, I wanted to ask you," said Kostya, thoughtfully, "is there such a book in which everything is written down—that is, the whole life's been written down—how to live and manage one's life ?"

"There was such a book, and it's run off," said the old man as he munched his bread-and-butter. "It was called *The Pigeon's Book*."

"The pigeon's . . ." drawled out Kostya, "the pigeon's !" . . .

"It was the laughing-stock of the world !" The old man almost choked ; the butter ran down his beard and on to his dressing-gown.

"Why should I live if I am to die, and I'm sure to die ; there's no joy in life ; I seem to be living without any reason," said Kostya, as he threw away the flower and, walking up to the table, looked fixedly at his father. "I'd like to learn to play on the trumpet, papa, but Katya's teacher says that I am weak and that I mustn't play on the trumpet. But there's nothing I'd like better ! I'd like, papa, to learn it on the sly, so that no one should know."

The old man suddenly contracted ; it seemed

to the old man's diseased mind that cow's feet protruded from his cup.

" Kostya, do you see nothing ? " asked the old man, trembling all over, his mouth all awry.

Kostya's eyes became even more bulging.

" Where, papa ? "

" Come nearer, you stubborn numskull ! "

But the cough, which suddenly gripped the old man's breast and rattled there, chased the cow's feet from the cup. The old man rose and, convulsively wrapping himself round in his dressing-gown, made his way to the sofa. He lay down and closed his eyes.

" Why live if I am to die ? " came the long-drawn out moan from the old man's heart. The old man's gaze was averted ; he was still afraid of the cow's feet. Memories came back to him —of his youth, his former health, his dead wife ; they came back to him as something very distant, and irrevocable, and it was hard to believe that it all had been, had been not merely in a dream but in reality.

The old man raised himself up on the sofa and opened his mouth wide. And he sat there with his lone, gnawing pain—recalling his remote past ; with his lone, gnawing pain—recalling his irrevocable past.

Kostya stood a while near the window and surveyed the long stretch of cold landscape, then after walking round all the corners of the room, began to descend below, his face pale as the moon.

"It's a dog's life," mumbled Kostya. "It's time to go to bed."

Kostya disappeared. Then Raya came into the dining-room, followed by the shop-assistant Motya, Khristina's brother. They exchanged some broken words with one another in a lovers' tongue, comprehensible to them alone. They drank their tea quickly and left.

Then came in Katya, a pensive, tired school-girl. She broke off a piece of bread, walked up to the mirror, looked into it as if she were being watched by some one, and grew sad. She walked across the room, opened the piano, but seeing her father, she quietly lowered the cover and went out quickly.

Then the housemaid Frosya came in. She hastily wiped the dishes with her strong hands, put them in the sideboard, slipped a handful of sugar into her pocket, and, snatching up the samovar as if it were a feather, took it with her into the kitchen.

Then the dog Koupon came running in. He sniffed at the old man, looked through the window at the moon, and curled up near the sofa at his old master's feet.

The old man sat there with open mouth, and did not move.

It seemed to the old man that black-beetles

had begun to spread in his ailing head, and that his head was already so full of black-beetles' eggs that they were pushing through. In great terror he felt the black-beetles' moustaches coming out of his eyes ; he felt the odour of black-beetles' eggs ; and he sat there with open mouth and did not move.

The old man resembled that terrible thing in human existence—the inevitable ; it watches on the threshold of every habitation, it sits before the doors of doomed homes and, on overhearing a happy word, opens a barely visible crevice for deaf, inevitable misfortune to enter in.

A cuckoo sprang out of the clock, and having cuckooed quickly, hid itself again in its little house.

The time went on ; the clock ticked off its moments into an abyss from which there is no return ; it repeated one and the same thing, one and the same thing, as yesterday so to-day.

Chapter V

KHRISTINA, now alone, undressed and went to bed. But she could not sleep. She rose, lit a candle, and sat down on her husband's undisturbed empty bed. And everything that happened from the first day of their marriage— every day that they had lived together—was recalled to her memory. The circle of harrowing thoughts once more locked itself in.

It seemed as if some one's hands were throttling her more and more tightly, and made it hard for her to breathe.

Khristina felt stifled. She jumped up and began to pace the room.

The candle burned badly, flickered, and little red circles swam before Khristina's eyes, and in these circles there appeared to hop up and down little india-rubber boys—Irinushka's favourite toys.

Khristina walked quickly towards the small bed : Irinushka, sprawling, slept there quietly, her little lips shaped into a sweet pout.

" My dear girlie, my own sweet, short-nosed cherub, you are asleep, you don't know. What will become of us ? What can we expect ? "—she suddenly straightened out—" No, I want to live. I will live—indeed, I will ! "—she clenched her fists—" I'll be strong, I'll break loose from the

37

accursed clutches that hold me, I'll hit back, I'll show them ; they'll try to bring me down, but I'll not yield. I'm still young, and I have strength ! "—she smiled bitterly and thought : " I haven't yet passed a day without Sergey ; to-morrow will be the first day, then will come another, and a third, and a tenth, then a month, a year, and still another year. . . ."

Meanwhile, behind the wall, the old man resumed his convulsive cough ; it rattled and whistled and snored : the old man was choking with it.

And it was as if, under her very ears, some one were scraping paper with a finger-nail, then crunching it with his fingers. And there was no way to shut out the noise, nowhere to hide from it.

She pressed her hands to her temples, her dry eyes felt inflamed, she put her hands to her heart. Her restless thought drilled its way through the brain, and, having drilled through, came in touch with a secret nerve, and, having found this secret nerve, it cut it asunder.

She got down on her knees.

" O Lord, forgive me, I cannot stand it any longer. I'll kill the old man. O Lord, forgive me ! "

She went on praying intensely, imploring to be forgiven for not being able to stand it any longer ; she prayed for Sergey, for Irinushka, for herself, and no longer knew what to ask and what to pray for.

She remained on her knees a long time, and forgot that she had been praying. At last she rose, and walked up and down the room ; half reeling in her fatigue, she paused, picked up things in an aimless way from the table and put them back again ; with an air of concentration she absurdly rearranged the books and the gew-gaws, now listened intently, now looked out of the window into the moonlit night on the moon.

The greenish snow sparkled. The heavy frozen mist, to be seen in all directions, also sparkled. Her thoughts, too, began to flash sparks.

"'A great misfortune has happened.' Who said that? Kostya. No, not Kostya. Who, then? Nelidov."

As Khristina recalled Nelidov she flushed with a sudden onslaught of thoughts ; for Nelidov was Sergey's companion and friend, and he would save her. Nelidov was such a man ; he would find the means for her, he would save her !

She already imagined to herself how, thanks to Nelidov, everything would return to its former state, everything would improve and go on as it should, and the picture thus conjured up in her mind caused her lips to assume a cooing, half-tipsy smile. Imploring, she desired. Yearning, she smiled. She was flaming in her sadness.

" Irinushka, my darling, my pet, my short-nosed cherub ! " She threw herself on the little bed, poured out kisses upon her darling, and as she sobbed her breast heaved high as with a great, flooding joy.

The candle dwindled, fed the flame, flared. Flared with a luminous iridescence, like a waxen, nuptial candle. And the little golden pendulum of the small antique clock ran to and fro—trembled, like a sprightly child, with spring tremors.

Raya slept below, in the children's bedroom. With a kind of animal fear she was turning over heavily from side to side, breathing with difficulty ; she felt herself oppressed by an incomprehensible weight. This weight, rolling, as it were, over her and dissipating in a shiver which tickled pleasantly, held her in a kind of torpor and released her again. Raya dreamt of an empty house. She was treading her way through its bewildering maze of corridors. She had walked through all the corridors and returned to the door, and there at the door she found herself in a small dark room, and sitting there in the small room she plunged into those secret reflections of a girl who falls in love with every man, and who has already received men's attentions.

THE CLOCK

As for Katya, she was turning over from side to side ; she could not close her melancholy eyes. She led her own colloquy.

She loved her brother Sergey and she knew well that Sergey was not to return ; she also knew that ill luck was watching their house and happiness was so rare—let but happiness open the door and look in, and it's no longer there, even its traces are gone. But she did not know whether it was like that everywhere or only in their house.

"If it were only possible," thought Katya, "to begin life anew ; if it were only possible to become small again like Irinushka, to imagine that in a few years you would go to school ; that you would wear a dark green dress with a black apron ; that many, many years would pass, and you would take a journey round the world and learn everything. . . ." If it were only possible to begin life anew, she would not begin at all like that !

Her lips opened, implored—Katya implored for the return of time, that she might dream of the dark green dress with the black apron, and that she might think, as Irinushka was thinking, that kittens were born of the wind : when the wind begins to blow—and to cry as she herself once cried because her toy cockerel would not drink milk, and because her toys, from the first to the last, the sailor-boys and the little fox, and the little elephant and the frog, would not come up to her.

There was a bursting, crackling sound outside her window ; it came from the icy wooden planks of the pavement. There was the sound of crunching snow under the window itself. Some one was frightening her, just as Kostya had frightened her before, when he pressed his face against the cold window-pane.

The old, unsightly, dusty clock on the wall, enclosed in its ponderous glass case, went on inexorably. And Katya's small black watch went on ticking in its place on the bedpost.

Katya listened intently to her small watch, and it seemed to her that upon these barely audible sounds, these slim, harsh tinkling voices of the delicate mechanism, she might penetrate into some deep place where all is visible. The little watch would receive her. The little watch would conduct her to the clock palace, where all is visible.

" When mamma was dying," thought Katya, " and her cry sounded through the whole house for a whole week, day and night, then every one knew that death had come into the house and would bear mamma away. Now Seryozha has left us, yet yesterday no one knew or even thought that this would happen. But there it was already known, there in the clock palace everything is visible."

Then Katya remembered how during the past summer, which was not so long ago, she lived with Sergey at a health resort, and there was a student there, Kuznetsov by name, and she fell in love with this Kuznetsov, and believed that she would love him to the end, unto death.

Did the student understand how Katya loved him—how was one to tell! But Sergey saw everything and knew, and not once did he offend as Raya had offended her—the mean, cunning Raya! or as Kostya had offended her and teased her—the mean, stupid Kostya! Had Sergey asked her about the student, she would have revealed her whole heart to him. How she did wish to reveal her heart, to tell some one about the student—how much she was in love with him, and how she believed that she would love him to the end, unto death.

Now Sergey would not ask her, Sergey would not return again.

She knew that well. And knowing that, she could not believe it ; she wanted to believe that Sergey would return and that they would again go together to the health resort, and that she would meet Kuznetsov there.

Katya's faith warmed her loving heart, and her heart began to overflow with the first virginal joy of first love. And it seemed to her that the little watch had received her, the little watch had taken her ; the little watch had conducted her

43

upon its barely audible sounds, upon its slim, barely tinkling voices, into its clock palace, into its very depth, where all is visible.

Through the window she could see the moonlit clouds passing. Like moonlit clouds there passed before Katya the days of her approaching life, and they were inundated with moonlight.

A dry crackle, coming from the icy planks of the wooden pavement, sounded outside her window, and it split the frosty air with a dull noise. Some one, very quietly, like Kostya, stole up to the window, and made the snow crunch. The moon approached the window, lit up the room, and its light flooded all objects.

There was a glitter upon Katya's little black watch.

The little watch tick-tacked, chattered, hummed a lullaby, enticed the virginal heart blossoming in its first love.

Chapter VI

A TIPSY crowd noisily and unsteadily filed out from the gay " New World." They were putting out the lights in the " New World," were preparing to pass a stuffy night. The musician was putting away his cheap music, the pianist was playing his last despairing note.

Holding up under the arm the tipsy Motya, the master goldsmith, Semyon Mitrofanovitch, himself as drunk as a fiddler, threw a kiss towards the " New World," and moved on with his companion in a bee-line down the street.

It was clear and bright in the spotted, greenish light of the moon. The trees decked themselves out with rich pearl. Their sturdy limbs crackled under the weight of their white jewels. While a dilapidated house with its black windows and grimy roof adorned itself with silver as in a fairy-tale.

" This same lady I'm telling you of has fallen in love with me," the master goldsmith poured out his maudlin soul to his friend. " ' Would you like to have some money, Senya ? ' she says. ' All that's mine,' she says, ' is yours. You can do with it what you like ! ' Good. I at once hired a *drozhka* with a couple of white horses, and took a ride through the park with her. Had our pictures taken together. Three dozen, cabinet size. All the same, I kept on thinking : she'll forget me—the jade ! But no, she didn't forget me, she sent me letter after letter, simply head over heels in love with me. 'Come to me,' she writes, ' or else I'll drop in on you myself.' And so I'd go to her. But I'm no fool, no molly-coddle. I'd let no one lead me by the nose. There's mistress Khristina Klotchkova, you know the sort of a mistress she is—a rotter ! ' Would you like,' says this same lady I'm speaking of, ' would you like a thousand roubles ?' Heh ! And her friend Pliugavka trying to delay matters and to force things, honest to God ! ' Senya,' she says, ' if you get tired of these parts and Palestines, if you get disgusted, or for some other reason . . .' "—the master goldsmith paused, began to rummage in his pockets and to throw out twisted pieces of useless paper, without finding Pliugavka's letters. " The devil, cabbage-head ! "—he called himself in his fury, and waved a hand as he gave up the hunt. " ' Senya,' says this same lady, ' take me, like a corpse . . .' "

" I myself have experienced life," stammered out Motya with some effort. " I myself went to St. Petersburg and that same night got myself a . . ."

The master goldsmith sniggered.

" The next day I paid a visit to the doctor," continued Motya ; " the doctor said . . ."

" Well, you are a ninny."

" The doctor said . . ."

" The devil take what he said ! Take it from me, old chap, I've had the same kind of cold for I can't tell you how long, and I spit on such trifles, as the devil knows."

" The doctor said : ' Young man, I myself have experienced life . . .' "

" Experienced ! " the master goldsmith mimicked his companion, " you blockhead, abomination, devil ! "

Motya was offended. With the intention of releasing himself from his companion's embrace, he drew out his arm, and fell headlong.

" You son of a dog, you son of a dog," muttered Motya through his teeth, as he made futile efforts to rise.

The other grew animated. With unusual care he put Motya on his feet, and, catching him under his arm, dragged him along with him. And, having dragged him to the very fence, he let him go down ; then he stepped behind Motya, caught hold of him by the collar, lingered a few moments, and, several times, with great enjoyment, poked the nose of his helpless companion into the frozen fence.

" Blockhead, abomination, devil ! "

Motya did not resist, his nose went on poking into the fence.

" Son of a she-dog, son of a she-dog . . ." muttered Motya through his teeth.

THE CLOCK

The frost on the fence began to thaw from the warmth of Motya's nose.

At last the master goldsmith grew visibly tired of this sport ; he released Motya and proceeded to cut the initials of his lady into the frosty fence. And again the pair walked on together peacefully.

Their shadows frisked in the moonlight. Now a shadow ran along like a dog, now floated like a ship, and then foundered.

The master goldsmith softened, and all at once grew voluble, as if he were pouring words out of a sieve :

" Well, brother, I once had an acquaintance, a postal official, Volkov by name, a man of gentle temper, but a frightful sponger. And this same Volkov manages to get hold of, none of your ninny cold, let me tell you, but something more choice, and even almond milk wouldn't help him. He walked about with it for a little while, then to get better he married—people say marriage is a cure. He lived with his wife for a year, then his wife ran away to her people ; as for him, he's played a real trick, honest to God . . . I'd come to him and I would say : ' Well, Volkov, how's your most faithful little dog ? ' And he'd laugh. ' I say, Volkov, aren't you disgusted ? ' ' No,' he says, ' that suits me.' In the end he shot . . . yes, both the wife and the dog. ' That will be enough,' he says. ' I've had my fun out of it.' "

" I myself have experienced life," interrupted Motya.

But the master goldsmith did not reply. They stumbled upon a policeman.

" We are walking along quietly and are behaving ourselves. What do you want from us ? " the master goldsmith said provokingly to the policeman.

The policeman was about to draw his sabre, but appeared to reconsider, and walked on.

" Well, why are you turning your mug ? Oo-ooh ! You dog-face ! "

" Senya, I say to you in good Russian, have patience, old chap, let's go on," sputtered Motya, afraid of getting into trouble.

" I don't want you to go with me. You can go where you like. . . . What's the meaning of this, if you please ? I'll not permit anyone to bump into me, the blighter ! "

And for a long time the master goldsmith would not be appeased. Although they had long since passed the policeman, who at once fell to dozing, yet he kept up his bluster and went on abusing now Motya, now the lamp-post, now any trifle that came into his head.

He suddenly desisted.

" Fresh, soft-boiled eggs. . . . ' How would you like, Senya,' says she, ' a thousand eggs ? ' "

" I . . . I like them soft-boiled," panted Motya with great effort, and furrowed his forehead profoundly, as if he were looking for an error in accounts. His eyes began to close of themselves. If he could but lie down now and fall asleep, and sleep to the end of time.

" A thousand eggs . . .," murmured the master goldsmith.

Having managed to drag themselves home, the two friends made their way into the hall, and though they did not intend to stamp with their feet or upset anything, they actually made a noise as if on purpose, and upset everything.

The master workman was dead tired. Motya was dead tired.

The awakened boy, Ivan Trofimitch, made haste to pull off the master goldsmith's boots.

" Ivan," commanded the master goldsmith, " cross yourself and kiss my heel ! "

The boy tugged at the tight socks, and in his sleep did not seem to grasp what was wanted of him.

" Ivan, cross yourself and kiss my heel ! " repeated the master goldsmith.

This also had little effect on the boy. Only when a hairy fist descended upon the small neckless body did Ivan Trofimitch humbly kneel, and, crossing himself repeatedly, kissed fervently the horny, dirty heel of Semyon Mitrofanovitch.

* **

THE CLOCK

Motya snored. The master goldsmith snored. Their noses worked like machines.

Ivan Trofimitch went out on tip-toes and, throwing himself down on the trunk in the small back passage, between the store-room and the kitchen, began his second sleep, with that reluctance and distaste with which, after having endured a hungry meal-hour, he might have begun his cabbage-soup after its third dilution.

But you can't get along without that, it's impossible to live otherwise—that is what the grown-ups do, he must submit to it. He must submit, endure. He was not a dog, he must eat everything. And if he didn't eat everything he would get it on the nape of his neck, perhaps turned out. And if he got turned out, where would he go? Where would he rest his head? He must submit, endure.

The small boy's oppressed heart mused under the rags :

"When I grow up, I'll buy myself a big watch, weighing four hundred pounds, with a chain, a silver one . . . then I'll give it to them!"

On the other side of the wall Kostya, lying on his back, looked terrible in the moonlight, watery somehow and stone-like, and he jerked his legs about like a frog.

Kostya had a dream. He dreamt that he had pulled out all his teeth, and that instead of teeth he had a match-box and the hard bone handle of a tooth-brush in his mouth ; as for his legs, they were cigar ends. And here he was, crawling on these, his cigar ends, into the mouth of the horn of an incredibly huge gramophone. It was a hard scramble for Kostya ; the horn of the gramophone was very smooth, and its sharp, metallic glitter hurt his eyes. But he did not dare to refuse to crawl. His hands slipped and he was already rolling backwards, but he grappled stubbornly ; moved a step forward and slipped down again, and he repeatedly renewed his efforts. Kostya was exhausted, and the horn began to contract ; it began to squeeze him, prick him, to tear his scalp off his head. And suddenly Kostya saw a hole under his very nose. He looked into the hole ; it was an abyss. He felt horrified ; some one appeared to be rubbing snow down his neck. Kostya hunched himself, made one great effort, caught hold of a cross-beam, but something seized him, and his feet gave way, and his hand could not keep its hold, and he fell into the abyss. And the master goldsmith, Semyon Mitrofanovitch, appeared to him to be holding his sides with laughter.

"Yes, brother, in solitary confinement."

The clock in the cathedral belfry struck three. There rolled by, one after the other, three prolonged, pensive strokes, three fore-ordained, ancient chimes.

And there was a deathly stillness upon the earth.

The waning tones, rising from the earth, floated and floated, and could not find their lunar shelter.

The cloudless moon barely sustained herself.

" Stop your pranks, Kostya ! " cried, the old cathedral watchman aloud as he dozed, and, straining his head upward, suddenly hunched his back and morosely began to pace round his beat, round the cold, white-stoned belfry.

High above the houses, at the topmost tier of the cathedral belfry, in the window opening, leaning his bony palms on the stone window-sill, and stretching his neck forward like a goose, some one was pouring out his laughter, while his wrinkled grey eyes welled with tears, and through his laughter and his tears he spat below upon the earth, in that moonlit night.

PART TWO

Chapter I

"LITTLE sun, lovely one, do peep out !" Nelidov went on repeating, as he recalled the nursery song he had heard so often at the Klotchkovs', hummed now by the petted Irinushka, now by Khristina, and he stretched out his hands towards the red-golden rays of the winter sunset which entered through the window.

His heart throbbed with joy—only a child's body and a child's word could radiate such joy.

"Little sun, lovely one, do peep out !" repeated Nelidov, simulating Irinushka's voice ; and he felt altogether near to her and to her naïve, childish invocation of the sun.

It seemed to him that this was the very thing of which he had been dreaming, and which he had been invoking all his life, for himself and for others, in the midst of the turmoil of incessant strife and pain.

"Serene eyes, tiny lips tremulous with bright laughter, lovely, little childish hands, and a body that is one with the sun ! Unless you again become like little children, life will not change, everything will remain as always—strife and pain and death."

54

THE CLOCK

"Little sun, lovely one, do peep out !"
repeated Nelidov in Irinushka's voice, simulating her way of invoking the sun—*the righteous
sun.*

No, not the stern one, which comes to chastise men—why should it chastise those who, even
without chastisement, are tormented upon this
suffering earth ?—not the cruel one, which, with
a sword, parts son from father and mother from
son, husband from wife and wife from husband
—where was the good in this, did not life have
enough partings and uncertainties ?—not the
proud one, sitting on a throne somewhere beyond
the clouds, whither reaches not a single wail,
not a single tear, not a single wish—no, it is
the sun, the quiet, penetrating glance, of gentle
speech, full of love and ultimate consolation :
"*Come to me !*" These are the words which
brighten the heart exhausted by deep suffering,
the heart touched with the sadness of inevitable
sufferings, the heart wounded by all sorts of
delusions, all sorts of distressing misfortunes that
mark the human lot ; these, then, are the gentle
words of love and of ultimate consolation, the
call of the righteous sun—*Come to me !*

The frosty winter day was darkening. The
sun was setting. The radiant blue sky was interlaced with golden threads ; there was the crackle
of frost—it sounded there, behind the darkening
distance, as if some one's hands were tearing

pieces of strong cloth. The shadows came on from all corners, quenched the flames, and turned the small purple clouds blood-red. Then the red-golden stains of cloud became dissipated, leaving only dark walls.

Nelidov walked away from the window. A sadness came upon him. After his almost child-like happiness.

Nelidov was but a chance visitor in Kostya's town. He had never thought of coming here. It was fate that brought him. An old friend-ship bound him to Sergey Klotchkov ; they had both studied at the same university and had become friends there. That was not so long ago. And in the course of a year or two all that one could possibly lose in life—all that, apparently, Nelidov lost. It was at this point in his life that he came to the Klotchkovs. His arrival happened to coincide with his friend's last happy day.

What did he do for Sergey ? What was there for him to do ? He did not know what to do even with himself. What could he do ? What was he, after all ? Simply one of a thousand— differing from the others in name only—a former official, actor, and schoolmaster ; simply a certain Mr. Nelidov, one of a thousand men of the past, present, and future, caught in the whirlpool of all sorts of worry and pettiness, seemingly exist-ing merely to go on jumping into scrapes and to get out again, leaving himself and others the worse for it.

But there had been a time when he was not like that. So he thought : there had been a time when he was not like that.

Chapter II

EVERYTHING around him became lost. The shadows, growing into giants, crept upon the earth, and shut off all light. The tree's boughs, as it were the arms of a skeleton, danced with the coming of the night wind. While the stars, looking through, appeared to swarm in the clear sky, as if on the point of tearing themselves away and flying away somewhere, in order not to look upon the harassed prisoner, the roveress earth, wandering in the great spaces.

There passed before Nelidov his nomadic life.

Yes, there had been a time when he was not like that.

He had had a fine, happy childhood. Then came a time in which he lived in great hopes. With all the fervour of his happy heart, he had believed it possible to create a new life upon the earth ; he had believed that heaven could be brought down upon the earth and that men could be returned to some lost paradise. He had erected for himself an impregnable temple of human salvation and had become the possessor of priceless treasures—all sorts of means for human salvation.

But soon his impregnable temple tumbled down, like a house of cards. All his treasures had come to dust. Some one had deceived him. He had deceived some one else. Afterwards he subtly argued himself into various things. Thus his happy time had come to an end.

And he began to feel a kind of fear before mankind, before himself ; this fear grew, became a cloud, shutting out every ray of light.

He slandered and scorned everything spotless, everything just ; rejected the trustful glance as cunning ; detected hypocrisy in affliction, and saw everywhere only the dirt, the slops, the dunghills of life.

And yet he still believed in his own heart ; it appeared to him to ebb with strength. That, too, was untrue : his heart proved helpless.

He had another friend at the university besides Klotchkov, a man named Feodorov, who was altogether unlike Klotchkov in character. Their paths in life lay quite apart : Sergey married and took over her father's business ; Feodorov, a strange, fearless man, played with death.

And so it happened that when Feodorov was sentenced to death, Nelidov put the strength of his heart to the test—Nelidov could do nothing for his friend. He was helpless by any vow of his heart to turn death aside, to hold back her hand, and all his words trembled on his lips as so many withered leaves on an autumn bough. And Feodorov's sentence was carried out. What should he have done ? Gone and avenged him ? That, of course, was not enough. What a naïve idea : death for death ! Would the death of the enemy, who had killed his friend, mend matters in any way, wipe out his friend's death ? What simplicity ! As if vengeance could return a life taken away. As if a heart —his heart—could be satisfied with vengeance ! Far better that he himself should die, taking vengeance neither upon Piotr, nor Ivan, nor Sidor, who would not care a hoot because you had snuffed out your life. Yes, it was better to renounce such a life, to make off without looking round. And he was quite ready to die. Yet, despite that, and his helpless, worthless heart, he did not die.

He could not die. He wanted to live a while longer. After all, he was one of a thousand— differing from the others in name only—a former official, actor, and schoolmaster ; simply a certain Mr. Nelidov, one of a thousand men of the past, present, and future, caught in the whirlpool of all sorts of worry and pettiness, seemingly exist-ing merely to go on jumping into scrapes and to get out again, leaving himself and others the worse for it. How was he to die of his own will, how was he to renounce life ! He saw this too clearly ; he knew the whole truth about himself and despised himself.

Could he but go to the end of the world, hide

himself somewhere, where no one should see him, where he should see no one.

And many days went by, unhappy days. It seemed to him that all the doors were wide open —go where you will !—yet he felt that, had he walked through any of them, he would have found nothing save emptiness.

But he must live. In some way he must make life liveable. And to make life liveable it was necessary to erect a temple for oneself and to believe in its impregnability, and neither to see nor feel anything else.

And in recalling those unhappy days, Nelidov remembered a little scene from life which, though a long time had passed, he could not blot out from his mind.

It happened on a day when there was good news of the war. Thousands crowded the streets, a procession moved triumphantly to the sound of music. A tram-car, surrounded by a crowd, was standing at a crossing and barring the way. A small, maimed dog was crawling from under the wheels. Blood ran from its protruding tongue, which hung upon a fractured jaw ; its broken leg dangled like a tail ; in this state the little dog rapidly limped away towards the cele-brating procession. The whining of the dog flew into the faces of the crowd, which was excited to savage frenzy by news of victory ; and it pierced through the cries, the music, and the shouts. That was not all. After the gay crowd had scattered and the little dog had died somewhere behind a wall, its whining did not cease. The dog's whining pierced the walls, entered the room, gnawed through the covers, flew into his ears, and there, inside somewhere, it pecked pitilessly, and with its sharp, poisoned heart pecked its way into his brain, then stole downwards through the warm veins into his heart, where it consumed every living fibre.

After that it was no longer possible to believe in victory; good news of the war lost all its meaning; it mattered little whether Russia would conquer or be conquered by the enemy. There was neither an enemy nor a Russia; there was only the maddening whine of a little dog, crushed without reason by a tram-car and left to die behind a wall.

As he recalled the little scene from life—the episode of the unfortunate little dog—Nelidov also remembered the strange dream he had had during the terrible night of the same day. He dreamt that he had suddenly found himself in the cathedral gallery. All the people below appeared to him to be alike, with similar faces, like a lot of Chinamen. He was standing in the cathedral gallery, leaning over the hand-rail, and as he looked down he could not tear his eyes away from a high catafalque which bore a high coffin, covered with a purple cloth. The evening service for the dead had taken place some time ago, yet the people did not depart ; they all appeared to wait for something, their eyes fixed on the terrible coffin, covered with the purple cloth. The cathedral was intensely silent ; neither sigh nor stir was heard ; only the red flames of the lustres burned strangely, as in almost audible pain. Then, suddenly, the bell rang, the bell rang as on Easter ; the loud resurrectional tones rang out. And as one man the crowd fell on their knees, their heads touching the ground ; and with a surging there came up from their bowed bodies, from the depth of their hearts, the shrill whine of a little dog mutilated without reason, a prolonged dog-like whine repressed through the ages. The purple cloth on the terrible coffin began to stir, to rise slowly. As for him, almost his entire body was bent over the hand-rail ; and unable to tear himself away, he looked down on that terrible coffin. Slowly the cloth rose from it. And in a single instant the cathedral grew lower ; and peering out from under the cloth, a monkey showed its teeth, and, after yawning several times, stretched out its paws toward the suffering multitude. Unable to sustain the weight, the hand-rail gave way, and precipitated him below, head downward. . . .

He then recalled another night, not a dog night, but worse— a blue night.

THE CLOCK

Nelidov jumped up from his place, and paced up and down the room. His frightened heart, as if assailed, began to beat fast.

That blue night. . . . It drank all his blood, consumed his whole soul, drained his whole heart. Blue, garlanded with stars, it gave no answer, and only tormented him.

Nelidov had had a betrothed. Out of his love he had created for himself an impregnable temple, but some one's hand demolished it to its very foundations : his betrothed had died.

In the dream which he saw on that blue night —it appeared to him that he was not alone, that there were many others like himself, whose temples had been demolished by some one's hand, and that these beings, tormented with pain, were clinging to one another somewhere in a place of execution, and that they had but one desire, were waiting for but one thing— death. Then he saw climb up on the scaffold, a little, hunched old woman ; and like a small child she clutched at the woodwork with her thin bony hands, and at the same time struck resoundingly with her crutch. "I don't want you here," she said smilingly. "Go to your homes, darlings. I have enough of my own. Come to me, all of you, in your own good time. But now you may go, darlings!" And she went on smiling.

No, his time had not yet come ; and he did

not die then, in that blue night. He could not die.

Nelidov paced up and down the room, and listened to the fast beating of his heart.

Chapter III

IT was quite dark outside. The trees, covered
with silvery tissue, looked into the windows with
darkened slender faces. The garden, covered
with white drifts, had a stony surface.

Nelidov lit the lamp, and sat down to read a
letter which had been just brought in.

It was Sergey's first letter since his departure,
and it was all very confused and desperate. It
was clear that he was having a hard time of it
hiding from his creditors. Sergey wrote that
he had reached his destination safely, but that he
could say nothing further as to whether he would
be able to endure his new dog-like life.

" . . . greet Khristina for me. Tell her that
I will write to her from my lodgings. I can't
just now. Tell her it's impossible just now,
really impossible. I don't know what prevents
me. I really don't know what I am doing.
For the moment I don't know what I'm going
to do. I do not know myself ; perhaps I have
never known myself. . . ."

Nelidov drew a mental picture of Sergey,
settled in some remote town, where no creditor
would find him, but where each day would find
him poorer, and at last penniless, a homeless
dog, who, in his detestable lodgings, would cut
his throat with a chip of a beer-bottle. But if he

should not succeed in putting an end to matters in that way, that is, if his hand should tremble, or he should be caught in time, then it would be still worse. Then, all sunk in suspicion, and delighting in his own humiliation, he would suffer and also make others suffer: he would be always attracting attention with his woebegone look, and would have quite the appearance of a cripple, entreating as it were for pity, yet trembling before any sign of pity. But pity or no pity, it was all the same; he was bound to take it as an injury and humiliation.

What was the difference, then, between him and Sergey? Nelidov asked himself. Was it not that Sergey did not know himself, and simply had never known himself, while he, Nelidov, had no recollection of a time when he did not know himself—there was the whole difference. Sergey could hide nothing, and would show himself to all, while he, having a knowledge of himself, could put a face on things as to fool even his best friend.

Nelidov folded the letter and was preparing to go to the Klotchkovs—to Khristina.

The door suddenly opened without a knock and Kostya's head appeared, all wrapped up in a hood.

" Well, how are you, Kostya ? " Nelidov greeted him, eyeing his strange visitor.

" So, so," said Kostya, frowning, and sat down without taking off his overcoat.

THE CLOCK

" Kostya, your belfry clock is rather prankish nowadays."

" It's nothing."

" What do you mean, it's nothing ? Now it goes too fast, now too slow, it's hard to follow it."

" Why should you follow it ? "

" So as to know the time. Everything, all life, is arranged according to the clock. Otherwise all affairs would get topsy-turvy."

" Let them get topsy-turvy ! "

" You will be put into jail for this, Kostya."

" In solitary confinement ? " asked Kostya with a smile.

" Solitary or not solitary, they'll decide that. They won't stop on that account. . . . Ah, Kostya, if all affairs were really to go topsy-turvy, if only there were no clocks at all, if time did not exist ; understand, Kostya, neither present, nor past, nor future ? "

Kostya suddenly rose, and, looking fixedly at Nelidov, asked sharply :

" Do you notice anything ? "

" Nothing."

" Nothing ? " Kostya twisted his mouth and, raising himself on his tip-toes, said in a low voice, like one gasping : " Soon there will be no time —neither present, nor past, nor future ! "—and, again lowering himself on his chair, his face grew sad, and he asked : " Where is Seryozha ? "

" Seryozha is attending to his affairs. Afterwards he will return."

" He'll never return ! I don't believe you, you are lying. . . . Vladimir Nikolayevitch, do you know, I too shall soon leave. . . . Really, why should I stick day after day in the shop ? The shop may go to the devil as far as I'm concerned. I'll tell you in secret, Vladimir Nikolayevitch, don't tell anyone ; yesterday I joined . . . the frog faith ! "

" What do you mean, the frog faith ? " asked Nelidov, and sat down near Kostya.

" You see, it's not so simple. . . . I've heard that you can attach another being to yourself, so that he should walk after you, like a shadow, follow you everywhere, always after you, and could do nothing without you . . . do you understand ? "

Nelidov lapsed into thought.

" You must desire that being very strongly, Kostya, with all your heart, with all your soul ; only then it is possible for him to follow you."

" Oh, I know ! " Kostya smiled condescendingly. " I have desired repeatedly, and it has come to nothing."

" If it has come to nothing, the fault lies with you, Kostya ; to desire in itself is not enough. You must have the right to desire ; you must have a strong heart, such a heart as would make even death submit to it. . . ."

"Don't say that," interrupted Kostya. "There is a way, a sure way. All you want is a frog. You've got to catch a frog and break off its left hind paw, and after you have dried this paw, you hook anyone you like with it without letting him see you do it. And the thing's done."

"What's the trouble, then?"

"The trouble is that I can't get hold of a frog's paw. . . . I have a hare's foot. . . ."

"Why don't you try that?"

"A hare's foot is quite another thing," said Kostya with a sickly frown, "that's used to avoid contamination, if you have a grudge against some one. . . ."

Nelidov began to feel sorry for Kostya.

"Spring will soon be here," he said. "You can then catch as many frogs as you like, and try your scheme."

"I need it now!—now!" Kostya trembled with impatience, and he sat there a painfully long time, all blown up, with bulging eyes, puffed up, like a frog, and his face became green, like a frog's.

More than once Nelidov began to talk, but there was no response from Kostya.

Suddenly Kostya, his mouth askew, rose from his seat, on his tip-toes, as before, and said in a low voice, like one gasping:

"Soon there will be no time—neither present,

nor past, nor future !"—and, shrinking within himself, left the room.

Nelidov overtook Kostya in the street. They walked side by side, one so tall and erect, the other so small and hunched. Neither spoke a word, and they walked in step with one another.

Thus they walked on, silently, with an even unhurried step, each intent on his purpose: Kostya—to overturn the world, Nelidov—with no other desire but to leave this world.

"Ah, Kostya, if only there were no clocks at all !" said Nelidov, breathing in the frosty air.

The fierce frost pinched their faces.

The stars were thickly strewn across the sky —gold in the king's garden. There the king sat with his queen ; the king was counting his wealth and drinking from his golden cup, the queen was stringing her starry beads.

PART THREE

Chapter I

KHRISTINA pressed her hands to her forehead, as if she wanted to shut herself in from the importunate, jarring outcries of the clocks, the creaking voices of the clocks—the walls of the shop were astir with them, quaked with them.

But the clocks could not pause in their colloquy, there was no way in which the clocks could control their unrest : they went on lisping, beating, knocking ; they importuned her in a human sort of way, and repeated again and again her newborn thoughts.

" A great misfortune has happened ! Nelidov is right. Now you are alone. It is hard for you without Sergey. What is there for you to do ? You can do nothing. Well, get to work now. You have a lucky hand. Roll up your sleeves higher. Go and receive your dear guest—your misfortune and unhappiness. Seat him in the image corner. Praise woe, so that it shan't weep ! —isn't that what they tell us ? But no more may you lounge in bed and think of nothing, or thoughtlessly indulge yourself without keeping an eye on time—precious time, without counting the hours. Time goes on. Time will not wait. No more may you linger while dressing your hair before the mirror, with no other thought but of yourself. No, you must jump out of your bed with daylight, and dress the best you can, quickly. You mustn't spend your time over pretty things, but dress merely decently. That is all that will be expected of you. There is much that becomes you. Do you remember ? Those two or three weeks in which you neglected yourself. Then your nails lost their glitter. But it will be worse, and still worse. You'll have no time, and you'll think it does not matter. Do you know what *no time* means ? It is as if a human being had fallen on the terrible cogs of the wheel of time, or, to put it more simply, on the little cog-wheel of a clock. The little wheel is inexorable, it will not let go, it will take hold of you and drag you along, it will tick in your very ear, make you aware of every second, it will weave a little singing nest in your heart, it will sing its song there. Everywhere the same song shall follow you, always the same song shall be with you, and you'll have nowhere to hide from this song : no time ! no time ! no time ! Take leave of your morning thoughts. It is good, on waking, to muse a little ? No, the old morning thoughts will not come, will not return ; do not wait for them. Besides, you dare not wait for them : you have too much to do, you have no time. Drink quickly your morning tea, then hurry along to the shop, and think the whole way, think tenaciously, one thought : that you mustn't overlook anything, mustn't forget anything, mustn't do anything that respectable people would not approve of. Respectable people, as you well know, have their strict commandments. Break but a single one of them, and you may as well wring your own neck. But you must not do such a thing. You must be obedient, you must submit. You have Irinushka, and the whole house is on your hands. Where would they all go without you—the old man, and Katya, and Raya, and Kostya, and Motya ? You must submit. You don't want to ? Is it hard for you to be alone ? Do you find it hard without Sergey ? Don't be astonished if you have offers of help. Only don't believe them. You are counted the first beauty in town. You know that well. In any case, all your beauty . . . It will not save you. When people save themselves from a fire, they do not stop to consider anything, but do all they can to throttle the flames. Is not life itself the same conflagration ? The fire, it is true, has long since gone out ; a deluge, so to speak, has put out the flame ; but there is the smoke, the awful fumes. The fumes steal over you, you cannot put them out with water. They are worse than the fire. You may look as much as you like here, you'll see nothing. Oh, only yesterday you failed to send to the bank in time ; the day before you were late in sending a letter, another day a bill. Meanwhile the hours ran on, without your noticing, and the bill lapsed. Well, never mind. Don't grieve. This business life will envelop you, its fumes will overcome you, and everything will go on swimmingly. And friends are sure to appear—you have many friends! Only don't believe them. You'll get into your head God knows what; you will succeed in angling a friendship out of pure civility, and afterwards, if things don't come up to your expectations, you will pine away, worry yourself to death, all for nothing. Why, indeed, should you? You'll have neither night nor day. Only a kind of twilight. One tooth won't meet another, that's what it will come to. Bitten lips, swollen eyelids, hands like leather, the brain a dead dot—all due to rage, despair, humiliation. Only rage and despair and humiliation. What is worse, you may fall ill. Suppose you do not fall ill. All the same, you'll die like a little maimed dog behind a wall. You remember Nelidov told you about the little dog? Of course, you remember. So don't believe anyone and don't deceive yourself. Your beauty—what is it really worth? It is only a delusion. Once, long before these troubles, it had some power, even fatal at times, but now . . . Of course, it is all right for trifles, *for a lark*, as Master Semyon Mitrofanovitch would say. . . ."

Khristina pressed her hands to her ears, as

if in this way she could stop her thoughts, but it was clear that this was not so simple a matter.

The clocks went on ticking, all the walls of the shop were murmuring—were whispering her own thoughts to her.

" Be brave, hold up your head, look things in the face. Matters will grow worse, and more painful. Your acquaintances are already beginning to turn away from you, they barely lift their hats, barely nod to you ; they cross the street to avoid you, fail to notice you, feel an awkwardness at the bare mention of your name. What should they say, since not one of them shows a nose in your doorway ? Why has no one shown a nose ? They have no time. No time ? How did they manage it before ? Why are they all so cruel, and no one seems to have a heart, but only words, hypocritical words ? Who has an interest in other people's troubles ? Judge for yourself ; have you any such interest ? But be brave ; it was you who said : ' I want to live, but I'll not yield myself ! ' You did say that ? Then resist to the end. Forget about the house, about the old man, about Katya and Raya, about Kostya and Motya, about Irinushka and about Sergey ; it's no good thinking about them ; it only takes your strength. Look how thin you have grown ; look at the dark circles under your eyes, at your wrinkles. In any case, you can't escape that. As for the old man . . . the old man is really ill ; he is not dissembling ; what was the use of pretending that black-beetles had begun to breed in his head and that a cow's feet were sticking out of a common tea-cup, and that black beetles' moustaches were beginning to sprout from his eyes ! Doesn't the old man want to give any money ? To come to the rescue ? Well, God knows, the old man has no money. The old man has managed to live through his life ; and you—will you manage to live through yours ? "

Khristina shuddered ; just outside, by the door, a man was standing and looking into the shop with a hesitating air and always appeared on the point of coming in. But, evidently, he had decided not to, and walked away.

A snowstorm rose, the white flakes whirled and whirled.

" I wonder why he is peeping in through the window ? After all, why shouldn't he peep ? It's so diverting to watch one killing oneself. Another's sorrow attracts and entices, and the one who looks on is pleased at the thought : ' Thank God, it's not me ! ' And it's interesting ; it saves one going to the theatre. People in trouble are so droll : they tear their hair, gnash their teeth, and make such faces, just as you've done a moment ago. . . . It's the same at funerals—you can't help laughing ! And you know what happens when, after the burial service,

77

they bear the cover to put on the coffin, well !
But why has Zatchesov stopped coming ? And
stopped your credit ? Or was it you who refused
his credit ? Do you think you will manage your
business better with ready cash ? Good, fire
at them your ready cash. But where will you
get it ? Don't the hens peck at it ? But,
really, isn't the earth big enough to hold us all ?
Is it possible that there is not a single person
who can help you, perhaps even save you ?
Is it possible that they are all like that ? What
about Nelidov ? What is hidden behind Nelidov's friendship and courtesy ? That is always
the case in the beginning ; then frankly—you
find you have been robbed of something. He is
Sergey's friend and is not like the others. That's
certain, quite certain. You can't make things
go ? Well, try hard. It is absolutely essential
that everything should be in order and bear a
number. And you yourself, what number marks
you ? You don't know ? But there are such
clever dogs ; they'll find out. Ask Kostya.
Kostya knows everything. He has entered the
frog faith. With a frog's paw he can attach to
himself whom he will. Number all these gew-
gaws ; that will divert you, make the time appear
shorter. An astonishing thing—time ; you remember how quickly it went that evening, on
the day of Sergey's departure. To-morrow you
must pay a bill. The important thing is that

you should not let it lapse ; don't forget, to-morrow is the day of settlement. Sergey used to forget. Sergey has tripped you up by his forgetfulness. Now save him ! You will be doing a good deed. Never mind your wrinkles, and that your jacket is hanging loosely. Save him ! And don't forget to send him money. Or else, you know what you may expect ; he'll take a little revolver in his hand, open his mouth, then aim and let go, and the thing's done. Who'll take care of him there ? Who'll show him kindness ? Who'll embrace him ? Comfort him ? Poor Sergey. What was he to do, poor devil, who's had ill luck ? To other chaps it was like water off a goose's back, but not to him. He'd lose at cards and forget about it. He's always put everything to his account. A gener-ous nature. His companions would eat and drink, and Sergey would pay for them all. The house was always full of visitors ; the house-bell rang all day long. There's friendship for you ! It was not even necessary to ask him ; he understood everything himself. Other people not only failed to offer help, but did not even understand, and waited until you asked. But you know what it is to ask. There are such friends whom it is necessary to ask. To-morrow you have a pay-ment to make, do you understand ? Ask Zatche-sov. Have you asked him ? Isn't he willing to give ? They've duped Sergey, they've all duped him. Do you know, even in the post office they sold him old stamps for new ones. But he has never deceived you. . . . He's at his wits' end now. 'I'll put an end to myself,' he says. 'I've brought you to this.' He is tormented with the thought that he has ruined you. Yes, and you must think about Katya ; these past three days have changed her so ! It's a bad sign —the pain in her throat. And don't forget the old man ; he sees cows' feet sticking out of cups, and black-beetles have begun to breed in his head. As for Kostya, a *zalezniak*＊ is going about inside him. Save, oh save them all ! Forget about yourself. It is all the same."

Khristina fixed her gaze on a single point and absurdly and hopelessly went on repeating one and the same thing, fettering her arms and legs.

"It is all the same, to me it is all the same !"

She was freed of a customer. He had kept her a long time as he chose things, priced them and bargained. Then he expressed his dissatisfaction and left after buying a small trifle.

The cash-box gained twenty copecks by the transaction.

Khristina counted all the money to see how much ready cash there was for to-morrow's payment. It was far from enough ; it was useless even to think of it.

"If she could only find a purse, full of gold,

＊ See footnote, page 21.

simply in the street somewhere, then she would pay everything at once and Sergey would come back. If she could only find a purse ! How little is wanted sometimes : she wanted a purse ; Kostya a nose, as in a picture ; and everything would be well."

The neighbour Zatchesov entered with an amiable smile and an effusive greeting. He talked of this and of that. He wanted to have a chat in private with her. Zatchesov would rescue them !

They disappeared into a little room behind the counter. Khristina looked at him with big eyes, and her heart beat fast. As for Zatchesov, he rummaged in his wallet and, picking out a bill, silently put it on the table.

But she could not pay it ; she had no money.

" Only scoundrels can act like that ! " exclaimed Zatchesov sharply, and his cry made a wall-clock tremble and caused its pendulum to fall.

Zatchesov put the promissory note back in his wallet and walked out without saying good-bye. And the restless striking of the clocks, and the garrulous songs which were part of the sound, sputtered as it were into her face like boiling water.

" Light the lamps ! " exclaimed Khristina in a harrowing voice, as if she wanted to unburden in her cry all the insults she had to suffer, all her helplessness ; to arrest the rolling hot tears ; and, having struck the table with her rings, she walked out of the little room and once more took her place in the shop, behind the counter.

A messenger handed her a letter from the bank. Again a notification—another payment due ! Well, what was she to do ?

" If Sergey truly loved her, if he had but a single drop of love for her, if he had but so much love for her, if the very tiniest bit of love, he would not have permitted it, he could not have permitted these affronts one after another. Yes, if he had only loved her, could all this have possibly happened ? He doesn't know what to do with himself. But was she any better off ? Yet it was she who insisted upon his going, for she wanted to save him."

" What do you want ? "

She addressed the question to a boy, who had been standing for some time before her and changing his position from foot to foot. He complained that a bill had been sent to his master Bakalov, which had been paid long ago.

" Motya, the book ! " shouted Khristina.

Motya, who was somewhat deaf, did not hear.

She once more called for her brother ; she was exasperated, and was losing her temper.

At last Motya heard and brought the book. They rummaged among the accounts and found Bakalov's. It was quite true, the bill had been paid.

"Sergey Andreyevitch forgot to note it down in the book."

"Forgot?"

"Khristina Feodorovna," complained Raya, "Kostya has again broken a window."

"Where is Kostya?"

"You are wanted at the telephone!" Khristina is bothered again and again.

The lamps were lit.

The walls grew animated: hung over with clocks, which eyed you with their large eyes through and through, and went on spinning their maddening clock-songs.

All this time the snowstorm tore at the window, noisily hammered at its framework, and stamped broad white leaves and white flowers on the glass.

There was a time when Khristina would come here, into the shop, feeling so happy, ready to smile at every one and to twirl round with every one in this swishing, snow-whirling dance of the white snowstorm.

It was time to dine. But Khristina lingered, afraid to leave—afraid of the snowstorm. The snowstorm would spring upon her, throw itself upon her, cut up her face, sting her eyes with its icy blasts. She was cold even as it was.

Rather stealthily, Khristina gathered up from the show-case a number of small, precious things, thrust them into a hand-bag and went out : they were intended to secure a loan.

A thousand bony white monsters threw themselves through the open door, received her, and, whistling as they flew, almost knocked her off her feet.

The snowstorm raged. And weep, or weep not, as you will ; there is no help.

Chapter II

"Do you know what I have done ?" Kostya dashed into the shop and, snorting all the while, began to get his head out of the hood.

Quite a pool collected round him from the melted snow.

Motya, paying no attention to him, went on reading in a low hoarse voice his *Key to a Woman's Heart*.

" When a young man, feeling himself attracted to an agreeable young person of the female sex, desires to conquer her youthful heart . . ."

" I've hooked on Frosya with a hare's foot," snorted Kostya, " and Frosya shook all over and grew blue, like indigo . . ."

Raya, quietly stealing up behind Motya, pressed her palms across his eyes. Motya helplessly turned his head about, and, freeing himself, ran after Raya. In the little room behind the counter something fell with a crashing noise to the floor, paused, as it were, for an instant, with a strained effort, and burst into a crackling sound ; Motya and Raya were tugging each other about.

There were sounds of face-slapping and hoarse squeals.

" You will upset the lamp ! "

" Motka ! "*

* The same as Motya, used in a more familiar sense.

THE CLOCK

" Let me go, do you hear ? "

" Take that ! And that, little beast ! "

Master Semyon Mitrofanovitch, dozing near the cash-drawer, bent down with an effort from his high seat and picked up the book dropped by Motya. He blew the dust from the book, and, like one unaccustomed, stupidly dividing the syllables, as it were, transforming the small letters into written characters, began to read in a touching voice.

Kostya, softened, picked up the chamois cloth and began somewhat zealously to wipe the glass on the clocks and watches.

" Lydotchka Lisitsina has become such a pretty girl, like a little flower, and do you know, Semyon Mitrofanovitch, she's getting prettier and prettier. . . ."

The master made a horrible face, as if he were about to cry, and sneezed loudly and formidably.

In answer to the sneeze there came rolling down, almost in a somersault, from the workroom above, the boy Ivan Trofimitch, and after Ivan Trofimitch, the dog Koupon.

" Did you call me ? " asked the boy, looking round.

" Call you ? Donkey ! " exclaimed Kostya as he threw a watch-glass on the floor, and, blowing up his cheeks and licking his chops, started for the workroom to get some tea, but after taking a few steps, stopped short and asked :

86

THE CLOCK

" Semyon Mitrofanovitch, what is it that gives one no rest either day or night ? "

" If you have a deep itch," said the master, sticking out his tongue, mimicking Kostya, " it's a sign that milk will become cheaper ; but if it's only on the surface, then——"

" Radishes ! " interrupted Kostya, with evident enjoyment.

Suddenly an awakened alarm-clock began its tinkling rattle. And the walls went singing on their unceasing songs, wearily, wearily on. Outside the window the snowstorm went on drubbing and thumping. A flame reeled in the shop-window, the snowstorm raged. And weep or not, as you will ; there is no help.

Motya, somewhat the worse for the encounter, pulled himself together, took up his place behind the counter, and began twirling his small moustaches.

Raya went on fussing before the mirrored door of the little room ; holding her hairpins between her teeth, she was putting her hair in order.

The master goldsmith yawned, and, slamming the book, *The Key to a Woman's Heart*, walked over to the gramophone and, having found some sort of " Persian March," started the mechanism going.

The sounds awakened, rolled out, as if bound, held together under a layer of dust, and they came on, pouring themselves out.

THE CLOCK

In response to the music the master gold-smith's thoughts poured themselves out.

Master Semyon Mitrofanovitch was thinking that now it was quite clear that his master had gone up the flue, run off, in fact, and would not pay him ; so would it not be a good idea for him to get away too, with his whole skin, so to speak ? It was bad to get mixed up in a mess like that— he may never get clear of it. He had seen tricksters like the Klotchkovs before : he ought to make off while there was a chance. Still, he mustn't chuck a good billet.

Something rattled at the top of the stairs, and following a shivering tinkle, there was the sound of heavy feet coming down the stairs.

" Here's tea ! " said Kostya, as with stamping feet he returned from the workroom with a tray-ful of tumblers.

The master changed the gramophone disc. Yes, he would get away from the Klotchkovs with his whole skin ; let them clear up their own mess.

They began drinking their tea. The little spoons tinkled in the tumblers, there was the sound of crunching sugar in their mouths—now they bit off little pieces of it, now they blew on their tea, and the gramophone droned on its tune.

" It weeps, it makes me think of Lydotchka ! " observed Kostya.

THE CLOCK

Motya, smiling pleasantly, said :

" I've never seen the Governor's wife ; they say she's an old woman, but very attractive. . . ."

" I'd let him have one. I'd let him know something ! " broke out the master suddenly, continuing his thoughts aloud ; once more he was annoyed at the thought that he might be chucking a good billet.

A customer entered and squatted down on a seat. The noise in the shop grew louder ; every one was talking at the same time, wrangling with one another.

" He's deaf," snorted Kostya, " happy, has his own horses, but stupid."

" What are you growling about ? " said the master with a wink, as, attending the customer, he looked among the shelves.

There was the scratching of a vexed, unwilling pen ; the deaf customer was taking his purchase on credit.

Again, as the door opened, the wail of the snowstorm entered in, as if it were intent upon keeping the deaf man from his liberty. The deaf man forced the door open ; the door shut with a slam.

The master put a new disc on the gramophone.

The restless Kostya, suiting his mood to the touching music, said rather plaintively :

" Semyon Mitrofanovitch, though I oughtn't to say it, yet speaking to you as man to man and not as to an older person, I must confess that when I see Lydotchka Lisitsina I feel somehow comforted ; my eyes have so got used to seeing her, Lydotchka Lisitsina. And when I don't see her I feel quite otherwise ; it is hard to do anything ; life seems to go wrong."

Raya, looking at Kostya, made faces and sniggered.

" You say it's impossible to leave the Klotchkovs ; very well," said the master, addressing himself to Motya with extended hand and bent thumb, and went on : " Tell me what is your rôle here : who are you and what's your make-up ? . . . Are you a trusted shop assistant, or just a sort of tolerated handy-man ? What will you get by staying on ? Aren't there enough jobs lying about ? They are sure to kill you with work here. Has that son of a she-dog bought you, that you want to stick to him ? "

" There are other girls, but I do not feel attracted to them," explained Kostya, continuing his own. " I don't talk with Lydotchka. I lose all power of words ; she is so charming that I can't think of anyone nicer in the whole world. I go out for a stroll, take a look five times at Lydotchka, bow to her and run off. . . ."

Raya, sniggering, bent towards Kostya and blew into his ear.

" I'm learning to sing, Senya. I've been training myself, you see. My voice is bass, like

Shalyapin's. I'll be a singer. I'll be a friend of Shalyapin's. . . ." Motya justified himself before the aggressive Semyon Mitrofanovitch.

Suddenly there was the sound of a sharp, vigorous slap; it was Kostya who had struck Raya across the cheek.

"Don't you dare! Don't you dare!" shrieked Raya with pain, while her face grew red.

Kostya, stepping backward, lost his balance, and bumped his nose against the horn of the gramophone.

"Crooked nose! Crooked nose!" exclaimed Raya as she ran to the mirrored door and stood ready to jump instantly into the small room.

Kostya was roused. He bit his lower lip until the blood came, and, seizing a gramophone disc, whirled it across. From top to bottom the mirrored door shivered, and there was a shower of glass.

The little pieces of glass came down tinkling, like light pieces of silver, and left rents in the smooth mirrored space of the shattered door.

Motya caught Kostya by the foot, and, flinging him aside, ran into the small room, where Raya was.

Raya was weeping:

"Motka, darling, Motka, it's hard to live here; he'll kill me, the beast!"

THE CLOCK

The master goldsmith, holding his sides, was roaring with delight.

" Go for her ; give it to her in her teeth ! " he set Kostya at Raya.

But it was already getting late ; it was time to close the shop.

Ivan Trofimitch came down from the workroom with a small tin lamp, which watched sleeplessly through the night, put it under the metal mouth of the gramophone, which was stilled, as it were, in a moment of yawning.

And only the clocks went on, as in the morning, as all day, as in the evening ; there was no forgetting for them, no sleep for them.

Chapter III

IT was Katya's second week in bed ; she had caught cold and had a sore throat. But the doctor said that the trouble was not in the cold, but in something she had inherited, and that her illness was dangerous.

It was Katya's second week all alone—who was there to think of her ? She felt all worn out, and her pain did not leave her ; she felt no improvement whatsoever.

"If I could only die !" Katya closed her eyes.

In the darkness, filled as if with dull echoes, there floated before her, cleaving to one another, the gleaming, sharp-toothed watch-wheels.

And it seemed to Katya that some one quietly opened the door, glanced at her there in the children's room, and walked away on tip-toes.

Then she heard voices on the other side of the wall. There was a squeak, a laugh. At first they spoke in whispers, then louder ; in the end sounds of laughing and squealing came in a wave.

"They've come back from the shop," thought Katya, "and they think I'm asleep."

It was as if a rusty vice pressed on her throat ; the blind iron pressed on it more and more tightly.

93

THE CLOCK

Katya wanted to turn her swollen neck, but its weight was too much for her, and, exhausted, she lay there inert.

On the other side of the wall they laughed again and again in a care-free manner. There was bitterness for her in this care-free laughter of others. She too once laughed like that, but that was so long ago. She felt bitterness in recalling it.

Her tears pinched, as with small claws, her weary eyelashes. She gasped for breath. There was not enough air. Air became so desirable, yet so unattainable. She wanted to live, but her heart bitterly said :

" If I could only die ! "

Again it seemed to Katya as if some one quietly opened the door and, coming up to her bed, bent over her—an all-hot being, who breathed hotly upon her face.

Katya tried hard to open her tear-stained eyes and to see who it was that was always approaching her and standing over her. But she could not. Soon it ceased to matter to her. A dull pain crushed all desire in her.

Then, suddenly, Katya saw her mother ; her mother stood before her as she had done some time ago, with a bandaged head, which she shook as she looked at her askance, as if reproaching her for her faint-heartedness.

" Mama ! " cried out Katya, as her last strength

left her, and another sleep without visions came upon her eyes, closing with pain.

Kostya, glancing at Katya through a crevice, sprang away from the door.

"Oh God, there's no end to it!" muttered Kostya, reaching out with his hands, as reeling, quite undressed but for his long black stockings, he walked through the rooms and up the stairs into the dining-room.

Chapter IV

THERE was light in the dining-room.

Before an open card-table sat the old man, not in his dressing-gown, but in festal order, in his short frock-coat. Empty chairs stood opposite him and on both sides. Two candles burnt on the little table, on the green surface of which a little path separated two columns of white figures.

" I cannot sleep any longer ! " said Kostya in a dull voice, without crossing the threshold of the dining-room.

The old man, preoccupied with the cards, continued the game : he shuffled, dealt out, threw out a card, played and winked. All hunched and emitting groans of discontent, he stopped to note down his loss. He drew his purse from his pocket, took from it a piece of gold, and, holding it a little while in his hand, timidly smiled and extended the coin—toward the empty chair, upon which presumably sat his lucky partner.

" I cannot sleep any longer ! " repeated Kostya, stretching himself to his full height on his thin black legs.

The coin jingled and rolled across the floor, then disappeared like a mouse under the sofa.

The old man, preoccupied with the cards, neither saw Kostya nor heard his voice. The old man continued the game : he made haste to win back his losses ; he dealt out the cards, shook his head, and, hiding from one imaginary partner, showed his cards to another ; then waited for something and whispered, folding his fingers into a *koukish*,* apparently taunting some one with the trembling *koukish*,* he shuffled, dealt, threw out a card, played and blinked.

The white pendulum in the little house of the clock cuckoo also blinked ; while the white blinds in the windows facing the piano now blew up, now fell back.

Khristina sat in her usual place behind the cold samovar, her elbows on the table, and looked with a mad stare on a black unshaded window.

The storm went on whirling, and the snow-drifts flung themselves at the window in black ribbons. Her thought travelled at times upon these ribbons, and, focussing itself on a dark point, returned to her in despair, and again departed. But her soul did not want to yield. And the thought, finding no outlet for itself, coiled up into a little cloud of tortuous thoughts, which, as if lifting their ravenous crows' beaks, spread out their sharp-feathered wings and pecked at her heart. And there appeared to be no place left for the heart, nor any outlet for it. Her

* Koukish, a clenched fist with the thumb thrust between the first and second fingers. This gesture signifies a great insult in Russia. To make it is as much as to say : "A fig for you !"

soul stubbornly refused to yield. And with all the strength of her soul she conquered her despair ; and alert hands appeared from somewhere and twisted the crowish necks of her cruel despairing thoughts.

In the meantime one of the old man's imaginary partners must have cheated—substituted a card.

The old man's face underwent a change ; a drop of sweat appeared on his wrinkled forehead. The old man jumped up, eyed his secret partner up and down, then trembled and, seizing a candlestick, lifted it high in order to strike the wretch.

" I cannot sleep any longer ! " said Kostya for the third time, and crossed the threshold of the dining-room.

At that moment the eyes of the old man, Khristina, and Kostya met. And it seemed as if the empty space that separated them became full. Their eyelids closed. A flame enveloped the souls of the old man, Khristina, and Kostya. They did not stir ; they stood still in their places ; they dared not stir in their terror and despair ; for, as if in reality, there were others in the room besides them—three partners sitting on the empty chairs, three tricksters, one for each of them, appointed by Fate herself.

Chapter V

IT was a hard, painful night. Kostya, returning from the dining-room, was afraid to remain alone in his room, so he went to Ivan Trofimitch.

They lay side by side on the trunk in the small back passage between the store-room and the kitchen.

The single-weighted clock in the kitchen prattled on insipidly.

The snowstorm hurled its drifts against the door and whistled; it swept the oven as with a hearth-broom; tore frantically in the chimney, then, as if exhausted, whined and moaned piteously, like a maimed little dog.

"Ah, Kostya," sighed Ivan Trofimitch, sorrowfully, "God has not granted me height."

"No, it's quite simple for a small person to get along even without God," said Kostya with a shiver. "But once you begin to learn, you get all spoiled. I too, Ivan Trofimitch, ought to be taller and shapelier. I take after my mother, yet my mother was tall. . . . Do you know, Ivan Trofimitch, I did not begin to walk until I was ten. I used to sit like a bug, or lie all stretched out. I had one toy—a small pig, made of clay, a little pig. I used to talk to it, and the little pig lay there and listened, the little pig. . . ."

"A small one mayn't even marry, they'd laugh."

"No one dare laugh, do you understand? Laughing is forbidden."

"What's the good of it being forbidden? No one would stop in our village for that. They simply won't let one pass; they'd call one an infant."

"I'd bite them if I were you."

"I'm not a dog, Kostya, to go biting."

"That's why God won't give you height, and you'll remain a dwarf all your life long."

"In our village, Kostya, when Prince Muilovarov gave a ball, they used to light all sorts of fires and made a kind of a sun-flood. Once the prince disappeared without a word; they looked for him seven days, and couldn't find him anywhere; but at last the prince was found, in a place where they didn't even think to look for him. Prince Muilovarov was found in a barn, like a beast, all naked, in a dog-kennel. He sat there fastened on a chain. . . . Just imagine, Kostya, he's fastened himself on a chain, himself too!"

"To kill your prince would be too good for him. I'd cut his arms and legs off! How dare he? Who gave him permission?"

"I've heard there are even worse cases, Kostya. They say, Kostya, it's in the breed."

There was a noise in the kitchen. Some one,

treading heavily with bare feet, passed down the little passage.

" The master," whispered Ivan Trofimitch, his heart faint with terror ; " it's Semyon Mitrofano-vitch himself, coming from the cook. He'll hit me one, if he feels like it ! "

" I'm not afraid of anyone ! " whispered back Kostya.

But the master passed by and did not touch him. When it became quiet once more, Ivan Trofi-mitch turned to Kostya and, pressing close to him, breathed straight into his face :

" Kostya, tell me, why is your nose crooked ? "

And the very same thing struck like an echo just outside the wall and, flinging itself into the street, passed from gate to gate, hurled itself far and wide, and swept round again and once more struck the two heads lying there.

Kostya did not stir.

" Kostya, you ought to pray to God."

Kostya was silent.

" You ought to pray to God, Kostya, about your nose."

" I never pray "—Kostya turned on him angrily —" and I don't intend to pray."

" Do you know, Kostya, in Byessinia ∗—there's a country called Byessinia—there lives a tribe, the Kourinassi,∗∗ with crooked noses ; and these

∗ Devil's-land.
∗∗ Hen-noses. Play on words.

same Kourinassi live in the sand ; they feel warm there and comfortable ; they lay huge eggs, goose eggs, in the sand . . . they feed on these goose eggs, Kostya."

Kostya flew into a rage.

" Goose eggs, and duck eggs," muttered Ivan Trofimitch with drowsy lips—" with crooked noses ! "—and began to sniff in his sleep.

The entire small passage began to sniff sleepily with Ivan Trofimitch.

Chapter VI

KOSTYA lay a long time with open eyes and listened.

Sadness gnawed at his heart. And the one thought of putting an end to himself, this one thought took hold of his whole fired being.

There he was—Kostya Klotchkov, who had power over Time and his hours, who forbade laughter and threatened the whole world with solitary confinement, who could chain people to himself with a frog's leg and evoke fear with a hare's foot—he no longer believed in himself. How could he believe?—the clocks went on as before, as they had done yesterday and to-day ; as before, every one was laughing at him, and Lydotchka Lisitsina was as far away from him as before. Why did she hide herself? Lydotchka would not even shake his hand !

No, there must be some other way out of it. But how? He would have sold his soul to the devil, would have cursed everything on earth, indeed, anything the devil would have called upon him to curse, but it was clear that even the devil kept away from him. He was alone and he could not manage it.

What had he to live for ? Why should he live? What was the good of living with a crooked nose ?

Kostya slid down from the trunk quietly—no one would hear him now !—and rummaged round. But he found nothing with which he could put an end to himself. There was nothing at all. His whole body shivering, as if scorched by the cold, he groped along the wall and felt the wall with his fingers. But he found nothing with which he could put an end to himself. There was nothing at all.

An unexpected and awful thought passed like a needle through his confused brain ; it followed, then, that since he could not find death, that he had conquered death ! A great rapture filled his soul !

" Deathless ! I, Kostya Klotchkov, the deathless ! "

This feeling of rapture in Kostya grew into wings, and the wings grew, and it appeared to him that they lifted him up towards the ceiling. Kostya lifted himself on his wings, his feet parted from the earth. And a kind of green light, painfully green, permeated his body.

" Deathless ! I, Kostya Klotchkov, the deathless ! "

" You are deathless, Kostya, and all-powerful," some one seemed to whisper to Kostya out of the ring of green light that surrounded him.

The light poured itself out greener and brighter, floated like a green cloud, and turning instantaneously into a huge reptile, plunged its claws into Kostya and chewed off his wings, and with a swing of its blazing-red jaws held him under.

Kostya fell to the floor with a noise.

Katya, on hearing the noise, sprang out of her bed, seized a little lamp and ran into the small passage, stumbling on the way upon chairs and groping past beds.

"Kostya ! Kostya !" gasped Katya, and turned back towards the door, gasping all the way back to the door of the children's room ; her undone cotton-wool bandages hung in tufts from her neck.

As for Kostya, his sharpened eyes looked with a motionless stare. He lay motionless at the foot of the trunk, like one dead. It seemed to him that the reptile, which issued out of the green, bright green, cloud, opened its flaming-red mouth and swallowed him, and that after being swallowed by the reptile, he rotated and rotated there in the cold, slippery reptilian insides, like a small factory machine, more and more swiftly, unable to stop. . . .

The lamp, trembling, went out. Katya, reaching her door, disappeared behind it. There were left only two in the little passage : Ivan Trofimitch on the trunk, and Kostya at the foot of the trunk—Kostya, rotating in the slippery reptilian insides, without pause.

*_**

THE CLOCK

It was a hard, painful night.

The snowstorm went on hurling its drifts, went on whistling ; it swept the oven as with a hearth-broom, tore frantically in the chimney, then, as if exhausted, whined and moaned piteously like a maimed little dog. And suddenly, having tired itself out, it sprang out of the chimney and roamed about in freedom.

The snowstorm shrieked and raged in its freedom.

It spread out its snow-white arms, clapped its hands, and, turning into a nimble little ball, started rolling. It gathered itself as into a larger ball, not really a ball, but a shell. This shell burst, shattered itself into thousands of flying little snakes, thousands of fast-scurrying little explosions, deceptive outcries, confused calls, and scattered to all the free winds.

Some one's steel nails tore the iron roofs. The gates rattled before the onslaughts. The call of the train stalled in the fields sounded lonely and homeless. The telegraph-wires droned, and their sounds wandered on. Some one ran along in chains and tore up rails, cast down posts.

The snow kept on falling and falling.

In the snow-swept field, under an aspen, lay a hare ; it cuddled itself under brushwood ; it did not know what to do, and went on folding its small white paws.

The snow-swept field was piling up with drifts.

THE CLOCK

From evening until the crowing of the cocks, from the first crowing of the cocks until daylight, there is no rest and there shall be no rest ; the storm has gathered up too much strength, and it shall dance on and not grow weary—it has been granted a long life.

And high above the fields, above the houses, above the town, in the high cathedral belfry, the clock bell struck savagely. Some one's long, sharp fingers turned forward and back, at random, the old clock hands.

And the clock went on. The clock struck its appointed hour.

The clock was unable to pause, and struck as if in consternation.

It did not know any specified time ; it did not know, just as people do not know, what will be to-morrow, what had been yesterday, where it will be, where it had been, who set it going, who regulated it, who appointed it to its unknown life—its impassable road.

PART FOUR
Chapter I

NELIDOV had become a constant visitor at the Klotchkovs'. He came in every evening to drink tea. He could not help them in any way in their business ; he had no money and no mind for commercial affairs, yet not a thing was done without him. Khristina needed some one to talk to about her misfortunes ; and when there was nothing to talk about she needed some one to be with her.

Khristina lived in a kind of tense fear. She would wake up in the morning with a feeling that perhaps it was better not to wake up at all. From morn until eve, she had not a moment's respite : every hour brought a new demand ; a new bill to pay that she had never thought of. She knew little about business ; only chance brought her into contact with it ; only chance placed her behind the counter. Besides, the Klotchkov business was badly entangled ; it was not even for such a man as neighbour Zatchesov to put it straight, though Zatchesov was a very clever man. Besides that, Khristina simply wanted to live, while the business enslaved her, and her fears and cares crushed her. She felt everything, and did not know how to free herself from her most bitter servitude, to which she saw no end. To whom could she talk about it ? To Sergey ? She could not bring herself to write to Sergey. It was true that he managed to get along somehow, if rather wretchedly ; he complained about it in every letter. There only remained Nelidov. He was the one man with whom she could exchange a word.

"If you only knew everything, Vladimir Nikolayevitch"—Khristina paused, as if she could not express in words all that seethed in her and tormented her—"you must explain to me !"— and she grew pensive, while her eyes implored, demanded an answer from him.

Nelidov was silent. All that he could say he had already said more than once ; and what he said was neither to the point nor of any use. Explanations were only entangling and irritating. How could one explain to another the most inexplicable thing—one's fate : why such a thing has happened to one and not another thing ; why all sorts of misfortunes fell upon one ; while earlier everything had been well ; why precisely that person and not another had been chosen for diverse punishments ; and what the reason was for it all. And Nelidov was silent. He paced up and down the room and resumed his seat.

As for Khristina, she was looking into her own soul ; and suddenly her voice sounded in such a way as to suggest that her words had not seen light before and were now being born for the first time.

"Life is incomprehensible to me when you are not here," she said. "I live and act as if I did not belong to myself. I wait for you ; and not so much for you as for your words. Perhaps not so much for your words as for your voice. I do not see you, I only hear you, I see another. And when I am hindered from listening to you I don't know what's happening to me. I can't recognize myself. . . . I am afraid for myself. Do you know what it means to be afraid for oneself ? "

Nelidov suddenly felt the strangeness of her voice ; she had never spoken to him in such a voice before, and he grew perturbed.

"Have I told you my last night's dream ? " He said the first thing that came into his head.

"No, you haven't told me." She looked at him as if she were ready to listen to anything he had to say, and, dream or no dream, it was all the same to her.

"I dreamt last night," said Nelidov, "that I was walking through a field. All around me was ripe corn. Among the corn stood some ramshackle carts. There were muzhiks in the carts. They were on their knees, their heads were bowed, their shirts were pulled over their heads. There was a throng of people near the carts who stamped the corn with their boots. Several muzhiks, distinguishable from the others by their wide velvet trousers, appeared to be doing a squat dance, and, with rods in their hands, they swung their arms with all their might to strike the bared backs of the muzhiks in the carts. Further on were more carts ; muzhiks were lying in them in their blue caftans and kicking up their legs ; they were waiting their turn. And there was such a low, dim-yellow sky. And I walked on from cart to cart across the field, and there was no end to the field."

As she listened to him, Khristina appeared to draw his words to her, and she smoothed her crossed arms as if she were soothing them. But he did not know his own voice. He only heard her breathing.

And strange shadows passed across their faces ; these shadows were alike.

A harsh cough suddenly resounded from the other side of the wall and sustained itself through a prolonged groan.

Khristina rose from her place and came very near to him—to his very eyes.

" My whole soul is ailing," she said ; " the old man is groaning ; there poor Katya is suffocating ; here this Kostya is walking about. I don't see an end to it "—she folded her arms. " Please do something, do something that will make things appear different, if only for a few days, if only for a minute, a single little minute ! "—and she pressed closely to him.

" Whom do I see ? " said Kostya, who entered

the dining-room unobserved ; he stood before them and blinked.

Khristina sprang back. And both Khristina and Nelidov began to say something, and they did not hear their own voices ; for Kostya saw and knew everything.

Frosya brought in the warmed-up samovar. Khristina took her usual place. Gradually she regained control over herself.

Kostya sat down near Nelidov.

" Guess where I've been ? " said Kostya, fidgeting in his chair.

Nelidov turned to him with a smile :

" Perhaps it was in the moon, Kostya ? "

" At a fortune-teller's ! " Kostya's eyes sparkled.

" There, take it ! " said Khristina, with a movement of her shoulders, as she held out a cup of tea toward Kostya.

Kostya paid no attention to her, and the tea spilled.

" Well, what did the fortune-teller tell you ? " asked Nelidov.

" There is a book of the planets," said Kostya, puffing out his cheeks, " the fortune-teller knows everything by looking into this book of the planets. One day a cooky who worked for a railroad director here came to him about her fortune, and so he opened his book of the planets and told her that she would be seduced by her chief—

ha-ha-ha, by her chief ; but she did not want that, so she came home from the fortune-teller's, got hold of something and strangled herself."

"Kostya !" exclaimed Khristina, striking the table with her finger-rings, "stop, do you hear !"

"Do you know, Vladimir Nikolayevitch," went on Kostya, "he's quite a simple man. He says that I have a star on my palm. Just look !" —he opened out his hand. "Now there is Seryozha . . . well, you know, Seryozha just before leaving had a whole box of matches go off in his hand. Now show me your hand !"

"Kostya, drink your tea and go to bed !" Khristina sternly interrupted him.

"Show me your hand, show me your hand !" said Kostya, trying to get hold of Nelidov's hand. Then he suddenly grew pale and pushed away his mug of tea. "I won't drink your nasty tea !" —and, all trembling, he rose haughtily and strode with heavy steps out of the room.

Kostya's footfalls had not grown silent when a shuffling of slippers became audible ; it was as if the old man were coming in stealthily to detect Khristina and Nelidov.

Nelidov rose. They exchanged glances. She looked at him meaningly and long ; he understood—without a word it was clear ; she loved him.

"Until to-morrow !"

The old man bowed to him in a humble way.

THE CLOCK

The old man grieved to see Nelidov leave so early ; they might have had a game together. He felt so lonely all by himself ; there was no one with whom to while away an evening.

" To-morrow ! To-morrow I'll come again, if for the whole night ! " said Nelidov on leaving.

Chapter II

A HEAVY silence hung in the room.

Khristina, after escorting Nelidov to the door, once more sat down in her accustomed place. The old man, having barely managed to drag himself over to the table, sat there all hunched up, terrible to look at, while his bristly eyebrows jutted out like black-beetles' moustaches.

They were one to the other as unnecessary objects, obstructions, from which it was simply impossible to know how to get away ; they were one to the other as a heavy yoke, a cross, come from God for unknown sins, seemingly for all life.

The old man reached across the table to get the bread, his mouth awry from the effort ; but he was unable to reach it.

The old man drank his tea without enjoying it.

" Do you know," said Khristina sharply, " that there is no hope for Katya. She will die here ; she ought to be sent away to the south at once. So the doctor says. She is seriously ill —you ought to know that ! "

The old man, fixing his glassy eyes on the sugar-bowl, made a wry movement with his lips.

" The shop will be seized, there's nothing to pay with, and something ought to be done for him "—she cast a glance toward the chair in which Kostya had sat—" he'll go out of his mind. Do you understand ? God knows what mischief he will do. Three nights ago he had a fit ; we thought he would never come to, and he frightened Katya ; it made her worse. Do you understand ? And his mind is wandering. God knows what he may be up to ! He will burn the house down, he will send us all off to the other world. I cannot do anything more. I have my own life to live. You have lived yours. I too want to live ; and I have my child besides."

As she recalled her Irinushka, with whom she had spent so little time of late, Khristina left the old man and went to her room. As she passed, she caught her reflection in the mirror, and suddenly blushed and grew pensive.

" Until to-morrow ! " She went on repeating Nelidov's words, " until to-morrow ! "

The bedroom was untidy and uncomfortable. Her heart tightened.

She bent over her little one ; she recalled how they had prayed together some time ago for papa, for mama, and for a little bird. And she smiled.

" Oh, the dear tootsy-wootsies, my little birdie, my charming pet, my dear little short-nose ! "

And for a long time Khristina stood over Irinushka's small bed. She did not feel like sleeping. But no sooner she lay down in her bed than she was overcome with heavy sleep.

She dreamt that she was at a railway station,

waiting for a train. The station was full of people. Some one said that a young couple was being escorted. Suddenly a door opened, and a crowd of small girls in white dresses, holding each other by the hand, formed a ring round her. At that moment the bell rang—the first bell, the second, and the third. Then she had a kind of premonition that she was too late and that the train would depart without her. She broke through the living ring of girlish hands, pushing the small girls in the white dresses aside ; but it was already too late, the train had gone. Then, in the light, she saw the movement of extraordinary images as across canvas ; it was like a vision of a procession—there were the same small girls in white dresses, and there was a bride in their midst ; but it was impossible to see the bride's face, for it was covered with a veil. Again the bell rang—the first bell, the second, and the third. And some one called her name in a clear and precise voice. Then she realized that the bride under the veil was she herself. And again some one called her name in a clear and precise voice.

Khristina shivered as if from a fearful shock, and as she opened her eyes, she clearly felt that some one was sitting in the darkness there at the table, and, no longer able to restrain himself, was weeping quietly and inconsolably ; he had come in stealthily and was weeping stealthily, weeping like one who loved and had not yet met a requiting love.

She was neither able to close her eyes again, nor stop her ears ; she lay there as when she awoke, all burning, and her heart in the darkness was conscious of something. . . .

But what could her heart know—her heart— has it not often been deceived !—her heart—has it not often deceived itself !

It was she herself who wept quietly, like he who loves and has not yet met a requiting love.

Chapter III

ON leaving the Klotchkovs, Nelidov did not immediately go home, but wandered a long time about town.

The light of the stars lay on the snowy pavement. And the street seemed to be a smooth stone road, continuous, unending.

The snow-dust, scattering like stars, swept toward him. The whirlwind came on with a shrill moan, lost itself, and came on again.

The wind sang passionately, neither lamenting nor sorrowing, and for Nelidov there was audible in its voice but one word, but one inexorable decision, but one will : *love !*

Some one, hiding somewhere, suddenly called him by name ; it was Khristina's voice that Nelidov heard.

Horses came flying along the highway. Their furious snore split the air asunder.

And the light of the stars trembled on the walls of the houses, on the stones of the side-walks and in his eyes.

The wind sang passionately, neither lamenting nor sorrowing, and for Nelidov there was audible in its voice but one word, but one inexorable decision, but one will : *love !*

Suddenly a struggle arose in his soul. It seemed as if the forces of his soul, let loose by

THE CLOCK

God upon his life, rose one against the other, strove with one another—those forces which move a being and stop him, lure him on to a mountain and push him off into an abyss, place him on a kingly throne and depose him to a night's lodging, give warning of sorrow by presentiment and deceive the keenest scent, dominate over knowledge and trample upon all knowledge, and, making game and derision of man, lead him a buffoon's dance, and afterwards compel him to tear his hair in despair.

The light of the stars, gleaming in his eyes, pulled, as it were, shroud after shroud from his eyes, and, dissipating the fog, revealed to him the paths to the hidden corners of his own soul, to all its unseen and unheard places.

His searching voice began to speak in his soul:
" You thought that you had been dreaming all your life long ; and, as Irinushka invokes the sun, you have invoked for yourself and for others the feeling of a peaceful, childlike joy, without which there can be no justification for ceaseless strife and death. You thought that the ultimate words in reward for earthly woes and all unhappiness, suffered by human beings, would be the words of the *righteous Sun*, words as soothing as Irinushka's joy, and full of love and consolation : ' *Come to me !* ' You thought that in order to live through life you must erect a temple for yourself and believe in its impregnability and neither see

nor feel anything else—nor to pay any attention
to the whine of a little dog maimed by a tram ;
otherwise everything would be lost—the impregnable temple would tumble down and Irinushka's
little face would become transformed into that of
a monkey, which, yawning, would seize you in
its embrace. You thought that your heart had
no strength and that your desires could not be
realized—your heart's strength could not stop
another's death ; you could not even die yourself
and you cannot die now, because you had been
caught in the whirlpool of all sorts of pettiness
and fretfulness, merely to go on living, you—one
of a thousand, differing from the others in name
only, a former official, actor, and schoolmaster, a
certain Mr. Nelidov, one of a thousand of the
past, present, and future—and you were always
right. You let only one thing escape you, something very important ; that, in reality, you had
sought in life and had seen in your dreams and
aspired your whole life long to secure just such a
thing—Khristina. And now you have found
her. Think of it, happy man, she will reveal to
you such treasures as you have not even dared to
dream of. She is counted the first beauty in
town ; she is truly the first beauty in town ; she
is a woman who, to her soul's depths, is such as
you have sought in life, have seen in your dreams,
and aspired to all life long—Khristina. Think
of it, happy man, she will give you strength, and

you shan't need any longer to do what you had once wished to do—that is, having changed nothing, to leave this world. Nor is there now any need to turn the world topsy-turvy, as the unhappy Kostya wishes to do ; and, without any exertion on your part, all that lives and struggles and creates will become yours and submit to you. Happy man, you will become a world, a tsar, and a god."

"A world ! A tsar ! A god !" cried out Nelidov.

And the same searching voice continued its frank speech in his soul :

"Sergey did not know how to value her, but you will know how to manage matters better, for you have a fine taste and a precise vision ; in an instant you will reveal the wealth of her qualities. You had once imagined that the only difference between you and Sergey was that while he had never learnt to know himself, you did not remember the time when you did not know yourself. How bitterly you have deceived yourself. What is your knowledge worth if you have missed, overlooked, the chief, the most essential thing in yourself—the very goal of your life—the very biggest thing in it ! No—you, too, do not know yourself, just as Sergey does not know himself, just as no one knows himself. Only God knows Himself, and the rogue knows himself —when he is at his rogueries—there are only two ! No—the difference between you and Sergey is that you possess the great gift of valuation and really know how to make a distinction between things, and only you and no one else knows how to appreciate Khristina. How could Sergey love her? Does one seek others when one loves? Just think a little! Do you remember how he once suggested a visit to the 'New World' together? 'Let us go, Volodya, to the "New World" and amuse ourselves.' And that was almost before the day of his departure! She knows nothing about it, of course; she does not even suspect that Sergey could be unfaithful to her. But she does not love him either; she only makes believe that she loves him. A woman cannot live without that; she must always have love, if only the appearance of love. And she truly loves. But you . . . do you really love her?"

"*Love !*"—the wind seemed to insist, and for Nelidov there was audible in its voice but one word, but one inexorable decision, but one will: *love !*

"I love her. I cannot live without her any longer. I love her!" whispered Nelidov.

But the searching voice did not cease in his soul:

"But suppose you should find something better, say younger, like Katya, as young as Katya, how would you act?"

Nelidov stopped still—a storm arose in his soul.

"That means, you do not love her. If you really loved her, loved her in earnest, so that living without your beloved appeared impossible ; then, only the Lord knows, you would not be troubled by the shadow of a doubt."

Nelidov suddenly increased his pace ; something seethed in him somewhere, perhaps somewhere in his very heart ; his whole soul was in a ferment.

"Do you remember why you came here and how you happened to chance into this town, and why you stood in need of Sergey ? You yourself have confessed that in the course of a certain year, or two years, you have lost, or appeared to have lost, all that is possible for anyone to lose. But what was your all ? You have been an official, an actor, a schoolmaster. If all the official institutions had tumbled down—that would have meant nothing to you. Isn't that so ? And if all the theatres had burned down—would that have mattered to you ? And if all the schools had been abolished—what difference would that have made to you ? But suppose it did mean something, mattered, made a difference to you. . . . All the same, you did not run to the scaffold— you remember the dream you had—there was no need for you to push your way to the scaffold and implore help of the old woman, Death. As

for her, the old woman, she was a sly old hag ;
she wouldn't have taken the trouble to send you
away and to call you a darling, but would have
simply spat in your face : ' Go, blockhead, to all
the devils. I have no use for your kind ! ' Are
you not ashamed of yourself ?—you have only
just remembered your betrothed, only now you
have recalled everything, only now your lips have
begun to tremble, only now your heart has begun
to suffer pain. That's how you know yourself !
That's how folk show themselves ! That blue
night. . . . You remember : you were ready to
bite the earth in your grief, and the earth floated
away from under your feet, and whether you
walked near a precipice or clambered up mountains, all torn or without a scratch, you felt nothing, observed nothing. Because there was nothing
for you, nothing to observe ; *she*—your betrothed
—was no longer. And you ran to the little old
woman : to beg kindness of the little old woman,
Death. But when she was alive, when she
promised herself to you, you will remember that
she appeared to you in all her radiance ; you saw
a halo round her head, like the halo round saints'
heads as drawn in the ikons, and there was not a
single little nook in her which you did not desire
to make your own. Yes, you wanted all of her,
that she should be all in you, yours in the full
sense of the word, one with you, inseparable from
you, cleaving to you indissolubly, not in any

mechanical sense, but merging as it were with you in a chemical sense, because you loved her really and truly.   But to love and not to desire to possess your beloved in that way is impossible. And to possess your beloved in that way and to destroy her—it was all the same to you.   You knew that.   And knowing that, what did you feel ?   What seethed in your heart then—what jealousy ?   It was a darkness to you, a torture, that she was, after all, an individual being, and that she could be by herself, could look upon objects, and that people could look upon her, and indeed might have certain thoughts. . . .   You remember how bright days grew dark because of your grief, because of your jealous, griefful thought, the thought that she was a being in herself, and this thought consumed your heart. You loved her, that was how you loved her, really and truly !   That blue night. . . .   Again you remember the hot July midday, when you returned from the graveyard, after the burial. You were overtaken by the burial party, who were also returning home.   They were being jolted in the empty carriage.   They had tired faces ; the collars of their white caftans were unbuttoned and showed their dirty dark cotton shirts.   They were hungry.   One of them, sitting on the cata-falque, was munching a roll greedily. . . .   And the streets appeared to you so narrow and the sky so low.   She was no longer.   She had died.   But

love never dies. If you love really and truly,
your love is once and for always. You may fool
yourself as much as you like ; you may stifle it
for a time ; but to root it out, to kill it—that you
can never do. Love will never die. But how
can you return her whom you had once lost ?
Yes, how can that be done ? You can never
return her."

" Love ! " persisted the wind, and for Nelidov there was audible in its voice but one word,
but one inexorable decision, but one will : *love !*

" Yes, there is no return ! But who can say
to himself, there must be no return ? You are
a lucky man ; you have met her, and lost her, and
now you are seeking though you shall not find.
But there are others who have never met anyone
and who have not been fated to meet anyone—
they are such indifferent people. And there are
again such unhappy ones, who did meet some one,
but had not the strength to take. . . . Khristina
is unhappy. But she is not unhappy because
she has no money and there is a household on her
hands—the old man, and Katya and Raya, and
Kostya and Motya, and a load of debts. It is not
a matter of money. Thank God, she has no
money. That house and those debts will make
her tear her heart out and unburden upon something all the weight of her heart, newly awakened
to love. She also has met some one, she has met
you. She has fallen in love with you. She has

fallen in love with you for once and for always. But you, you do not love her—what, then, do you want? For the last time I say, what do you want?

"Love!" the wind seemed to persist; for Nelidov there was audible in its voice but one word, but one inexorable decision, but one will: *love!*

Again the furious snore split the air; horses came flying along the highway. And the light of the stars trembled on the walls of the houses, on the stones of the side-walks, and in his eyes.

And all night long Nelidov wandered in the deserted streets on the stone road—a road that seemed continuous, unending.

It stretched before him as if it were alive. He could hear its heart. And his own heart went on beating and beating, as if it desired to beat its way through to freedom.

The snow-dust, scattering like stars, swept toward him.

The stars and the wind.

The starry sky shone peacefully with a halo. There the Immaculate Virgin—the Mother of God—was sewing a silken shroud, a godly vestment. She was putting spangles in the middle and embroidery on the edges. Three angels, three silver ones, shaded the Immaculate Virgin, the Mother of God, with their wings. The starry sky shone peacefully with a halo.

PART FIVE

Chapter I

IT was becoming clear that the doctors could not provide the crimson lanterns with which it is possible to drive away that most horrible and evil misfortune—smallpox. Or was it that Katya was beyond the help of all kinds of lanterns, even though you lit a hundred, whether crimson or any other kindred colour?

The illness, growing from day to day, was consuming Katya.

Poor sweet Katya—hapless girl! She had never spoken her secret, passionate, girlish words; she had never poured out her loving heart, full of well-springs, which, seething, were ready to overflow and to brighten the whole world with its light.

The pale light of a new dawn entered the children's room through the small snow-wrapt window. But when the sun shall look out and the snow round the window begin to thaw, there will be no more Katya.

Poor sweet Katya—hapless girl! Who, then, was to blame for her cruel fate, for her approaching incomprehensible and needless death? The old man, her father, loved her; the old man did not want her to die. It all just happened like that. Sometime, in the long ago, soon after his marriage, the old man went on business to St. Petersburg, and the very first day of his stay in St. Petersburg he, like Motya, after a merry diversion with a nocturnal dame from Nevsky Prospect, had an illness. Could he then have foreseen anything? Could he have thought of the unhappy consequences? No, the old man was not at all to blame. Who, then, in the end of things, was to blame?

Soon the spring would be here, soon the sun would peep out, but Katya shall see neither the spring nor the sun. She will be taken South— to a warm land. The doctors said that she ought to be taken at once to a warm land. Perhaps she will improve there, perhaps she will return. . . . Of course, everything is possible !

Poor sweet Katya—hapless girl !

Katya was dozing in her deep arm-chair.

Her large eyes were intensely spiritual, there was not a drop of blood in them, while her sharp eyebrows appeared black across the stretched skin like two black watch-hands which had paused at twenty minutes past eight. She was quite unlike her former self, and the rings on her now lean fingers looked conspicuous and out of place and almost slipped off.

Her large eyes were deeply thoughtful, but her thoughts were calm, passed the bounds of life, and with every hour approached nearer to something different, losing their habitual speech.

Katya could not make them out. A deep indifference permeated all her being.

Katya wanted nothing, nothing interested her, nothing held her, as if there were nothing in her soul, simply nothing, which she might recall and muse and grieve about a little. She remembered neither her yesterdays, nor the summer resort, nor the student Kuznetsov, nor her brother Sergey. What mattered it now that the snow was falling just outside her window, or that her skates hung in the corner of the room—it was all the same to her now.

Katya's small black watch ticked on a post of her bed—it whispered on peacefully and faithfully from hour to hour ; its course had been measured out, and it had nothing to worry about.

A feast-day came. Tarts were being baked at the Klotchkovs', and the smell of tarts and of roast meat came from the kitchen ; the fat smell of the edibles settled poignantly in Katya's mouth, somewhere on her tongue.

The house was desolate, the old man slept. Kostya alone restlessly paced overhead, and his footfalls sounded like dull hammer-beats ; and Niusha, the cook, tearing herself away from the stove, would run in now and then to inquire. But Niusha also disappeared somewhere—she went to the cellar for a cabbage ; the footsteps above also died away.

THE CLOCK

The snow, falling, spread its powder across the window and took away what little light there was.

It was midday, but it looked like twilight.

The door of the children's room quietly opened. Glancing restlessly round, an unknown woman, her head covered with a kerchief, entered the children's room.

Katya wanted to greet her, but her tongue refused to stir, and only her lips, grimacing, faintly smiled.

"It must be the nurse who is to take me to a warm country," thought Katya, comforted.

The unknown woman—the *nurse*—showing no haste, sat down opposite Katya.

"It is time, my girl," said the nurse, "it is time to start the journey, to the warm country. It is so warm and so good there. Ah, so good, dear girl, that it is hard merely to imagine it. There is nothing of that here ; you can't even breathe properly here, my dear girl."

Katya looked into the face of the unknown woman—her nurse—and it seemed to her that she had seen her once before, but she could not remember where she had seen her.

"It is spring there, dear girl, always spring. And when God grants your return, and you are back here once more, you will be quite another being, an altogether radiant being . . ."—the nurse's voice stopped short ; she stretched out her hand toward the bed-post, deftly snatched Katya's small black watch, and clutching the watch in her hand, she rose, so proud and so tall, from the chair, and, swinging her arms, she threw the watch on the floor—" there's nothing of the sort there ! "

Katya trembled like a leaf ; from under the nurse's slipping kerchief she could see a tightly drawn white bandage, such as her dead mother had worn.

" There's nothing of the sort there !   There's no time there ! "—and, stamping the floor with her heel, the nurse smashed the watch.

And the pale, barely perceptible light, which entered the children's room through the small snow-wrapt window, became extinguished.

" Katya, Katyechka, what is the matter with you ? "—Khristina, who had returned from Mass to find Katya in a deep swoon, got down on her knees and took Katya's hand.

Katya, recovering consciousness, was crying quietly, like a suppliant.

" We will start to-day, Katyechka ; we will start to-day for the warm country. It is good there, it is warm there. If you like, I'll go with you."

" No ! " said Katya, trembling all over. " No, Khristina, it is not time for you yet ! "

" Well, be good, Katya ; to-day is your birth-day. You have my good wishes ! "

THE CLOCK

Katya was crying quietly, like a suppliant.

She was beginning to hear her quiet thoughts, and to understand them, and her quiet thoughts were crossing the last boundary of life and were revealing to her their other voice, understood by her for the first time.

The small black watch on the bed-post had ceased ticking and stood still.

Chapter II

THAT whole afternoon was spent by the Klotchkovs in preparation for the holiday.

A stranger would have thought that a great happiness had come into the house. For some reason every one was frightfully gay, and, in spite of an effort to appear reticent, could not hide his joy.

Irinushka went off into a cackle, like a little hen ; the deaf Motya sang, reaching out higher and higher toward incredible bird-like heights ; Raya helped him—her scant voice trilled with a squeak that seemed to come from the bowels ; and both, as if angry, suddenly set up a hysterical roar, which sounded not unlike a horse's neighing.

Khristina, in a holiday mood, dressed herself in a way that was especially becoming ; in her soft fluffy jacket she appeared as the sun giving colour to a misty, snowy day.

Kostya, gloomy and restless from the time he rose from his bed, became insolent and unmanageable. His face appeared to drop its mask, and he was all tousy and untidy and irritable ; his words poured out with an ape-like cackle, in such profusion that you could have heaped them up into a cart. Every now and then he took a small secret box from his pocket and, opening its cover, let out, unobserved, some fleas, both human fleas and dog fleas, collected by him through many months for his own ends, which were wholly a mystery to every one.

The red-faced Frosya, worried by Motya and by Kostya, screeched like a samovar and snarled and struck out wildly with her arms to repay for their rather brutal pleasantries, but chiefly for their tearing her new jacket.

And the old man, bristling, his hair sticking out as if glued on, attired in his greasy brown dressing-gown with none of its buttons fastened, his body all in poultices, now grimaced strangely, now twitched owing to the pinching poultices, and shook his newspaper under the snorts, pranks, and unceasing sallies made by Kostya.

The unhappy piano, put out of tune and dulled by the dull playing of dull pieces, drummed on incessantly, while the paper ornaments of the candlesticks jumped up and down as if half-witted.

The dog Koupon was restless, and howled and whined. And Kostya's hungry fleas, human and dog fleas, let free once more, hopped about and bit every one ; they also bit Kostya.

Then dinner was ready—every one sat down at the table ; the din did not cease. The table was set in holiday order, with bottles—such a dinner was not seen in the house since Sergey's departure. And all this was on the occasion of Katya's birthday and departure.

THE CLOCK

They waited for Nelidov, the one and constant visitor at the Klotchkovs'. Every one jumped up when the bell rang. But instead of Nelidov the master goldsmith, Semyon Mitrofanovitch, appeared in the dining-room.

A hubbub arose, the walls trembled.

It is true, the master goldsmith's appearance was terrible; there was something incredible in his negligence, due, no doubt, not so much to great haste as to some perturbation. From under his smart swallow-tail coat there hung the tail of his untucked-in shirt.

Semyon Mitrofanovitch appeared with the definite decision of announcing his resignation and of demanding a settlement, but, disturbed by the unusual welcome, he succumbed to the vodka and postponed action.

The dinner progressed in its proper order.

Kostya, in his irritation, upset a plate of vermicelli on his own head, and moved towards his neighbours so as to annoy them with the pieces which stuck to him.

Raya had moved her chair so close to Motya's that she no longer sat on the chair but on Motya's knees; her face was covered with blushes, and she laughed shrilly.

The vodka was taking effect. It made the master goldsmith tipsy in a touching way. He acted like a tipsy woman; he began narrating and got badly mixed up: he started to tell his stories in the third person, but passed now and again to the first person, and gradually grew more and more vague and piled horror on horror, and lied, and himself disclosed his lies, and immediately afterwards began his babble anew. And for some reason, cutting his stories short in the middle, as if he had suddenly grown conscious of himself, he gave his whole attention to Khristina, hinting mysteriously, as he dug his hands deep into his bulging pockets and smiled not altogether decorously, but rather slyly.

The old man made most of this ; he ate greedily and beamed with pleasure as he munched away.

Koupon also profited ; Kostya let Koupon lick his hands.

Even Katya, carried upstairs from the children's room and forgetting herself in her deep arm-chair, became, as it were, the Katya of old and went on musing upon what would happen next month, in the summer to come, and the next year. . . . And only when the cuckoo, jumping from its clock-house, cuckooed, and every one got up from the table and made haste to accompany Katya to the station to see her off for the warm country, did Katya begin to cry.

She cried quietly, like a suppliant.

She knew.

And as she bade farewell and kissed Khristina,

THE CLOCK

Irinushka, the old man, her father, her sister Raya and her brother Kostya, and wished them happiness ; she knew.   She knew what they did not yet know about themselves.

And she cried quietly, like a suppliant.

Chapter III

A QUIET settled upon the house, and something else entered it—that peculiar and painful something which is present only after a death— a kind of emptiness. . . .

Frosya brought the samovar into the dining-room, put it on the table, and sobbed out as she turned to go. Frosya was so sorry for Katya, the poor girl !

" But why should I feel sorry ? " The country woman, her hair dressed like Raya's, at that moment reproached herself. " After all, she hasn't gone away to die. With God's help she'll get better, only that dust on the lips. . . . That's sad ! God's will be done ! " And she went to join Niusha in the kitchen.

The old man acted as master of the house. The old man saw to things ; there were such odd moments.

" Kostya, it would be better if you sang something decent, instead of humming away at random the way you are doing ! " said the old man, as he was piling on expensive soft caviare on a crust of black bread.

" Papa, I cannot sing such songs. I can sing only thieves' songs. . . . Tell me, papa, why does the *zalyezniak** go about my insides and

* See footnote, page 21.

scratch away at me with his nails, and why can't I sleep and everything is so disgusting to me ? "

" The tapeworm has got into you."

" The tapeworm ? "

" Well, a worm if you like ; you'd better examine it more attentively and bring it to me ! We'll give the dear chap a warm reception. Whether a worm or a tapeworm—it's all the same thing."

" The same thing . . ." repeated Kostya, and lapsed into thought. " But tell me, papa, what does the devil look like ? "

" The devil is black."

" Hah ! " snorted Kostya, " black ! But I saw him in a dream, papa, and do you know, papa, he was not at all black, not at all, and he had neither horns nor tail, and you could recognize him at once. He is afraid of nothing, and he is so quiet. You could look right through him ; you could see straight through him as through a net."

" If you'd sleep better you'd see nothing. Just try a mustard poultice ; it'll pinch you a bit, but it'll do you good."

" And what do you dream of, papa ? "

" What do I dream of ? I dream of apples. Lately I've dreamt of dried perch—three perches. Sometimes I dream of you, sometimes of Katya, and what not ! "

" Is it true, papa, that if you've dreamt that

something has happened to you, something unpleasant, it means you'll come into money?"

"Money! To be sure! Without fail!" said the old man, sucking a sugar-candy. "On the very eve of the day that I won twenty thousand roubles, I dreamt that I was sitting up there, d'you understand, and I sat scooping up as with the hollow of my hand, while your dead mother appeared to sit on the slop-pail."

"And we shall drown the kittens to-morrow in the slop-pail. Mariushka has just given birth to seven kittens." And Kostya gulped with pleasure.

The old man drew a doleful face, while his eyebrows bristled up like black-beetles' moustaches.

"That would be stupid, my boy. You'd better drown them in water, because they are little ones, tiny blind ones, and they'll feel cold. Try warm water"—and, choking, the old man clutched feverishly at his heart, while from the aching spot there came, as through several inflammations, the dragging, persistent sounds which combined a hoarse cackle, a whistle, a snore, and a cough.

Kostya walked restlessly up and down, went up to the piano, opened it, and began to strike a single key with one finger. He went on striking the single note for a long time, then slammed down the cover and descended below.

Hardly a minute had passed before Kostya returned.

THE CLOCK

" I'm afraid, papa," he said, not in his own voice.

The frail old man lay quietly on the sofa.

" I'm afraid," Kostya repeated, " there in the children's room, in front of Katya's table, some one is sitting. . . ."

" Let him sit," groaned the old man, breathing heavily ; " he will sit a while and go away."

The cuckoo jumped from its tiny clock-house and cuckooed the hours, hour after hour.

And there was a silence in the house ; and there was besides that peculiar and painful something which is present only after a death—a kind of emptiness.

Chapter IV

ON leaving the railway station, Khristina did not go home, but turned into another street, toward Nelidov's house.

She could no longer live a day without him, and her heart flamed from day to day, from meeting to meeting, from glance to glance. Anxiety sometimes seized her. What could be the matter? Why hasn't he come? Was he well?

And in truth Nelidov was not quite well; his eyes shone with a dry gleam, as if they were already seeing the inexorable before them, while from the depths of his eyes one tormenting thought looked out persistently.

She began with Katya, but that was only incidental to the rest that Khristina had to say about her affairs, about the house and the shop.

These outer cares had become for her a corner where she could hide herself for many hours, and a thing upon which it was so easy to relieve her heart.

"The old man doesn't want even to listen. He goes on saying the same thing over again, that he has no money and he won't budge; it's a matter only of days before we're sold out by the law."

"What's the matter with Sergey? It seems a long time since he has written."

THE CLOCK

" Sergey ! The shop will be sold out, then Sergey will show up. . . . But tell me, why is it, why, when misfortune comes, then everything and every one, as if conspiring together, desert one . . .? Isn't that always so ?"

" Misfortune has its own truth, just as love has its own truth. If you love . . ."

" If you love . . ." repeated Khristina after him as one repeats after the priest the prayer before Communion : *I believe, O Lord, and I confess . . .*

" If you love," went on Nelidov, " and are not loved in return, you are lost. It is of no matter, but you are lost. Everything will conspire at that moment ; all sorts of misfortunes will come ; and you'll slip on the smoothest place. Here is a case of a man being tried for murder : he has killed some one because he was insulted. But the truth of the matter is, that he did not kill because he had been insulted ; he would have never felt himself insulted if he had not felt himself oppressed by unrequited love. If you love and are not loved in return, you are lost. But to love another means to want another completely ; it is to want to make another all his own, to the very last nook. But the other remains a being in himself, separate from you, and this being sees and hears and thinks. I love you and I look at you, but you are pensive at this moment. . . . What are you thinking about ? I ask

145

myself. And I have an answer ready for myself. Yes, you have remembered something from your past, from your yesterdays lived without me, or you are occupied with a thought unknown to me—and that is enough for me. I see you severed from me, and I know that it cannot be otherwise, that you cannot be, all of you, my very own ; and I cannot accept the fact. To love and not to want to possess one's beloved in that way is impossible. But to possess a person in that way and to destroy that person comes to the same thing in the end."

She stood before him as one condemned, and all her blood, rushing to her heart, hid itself there, to rush back suddenly to her face, like a flame. She repeated his words, as she used to repeat the prayer uttered by the priest before Communion : *I believe, O Lord, and I confess.* . . .

His eyes shone with a dry gleam as if they already were seeing the inevitable before him, while from the depths of his eyes one tormenting thought looked out persistently. He felt that he loved Khristina and that he could not live without her, and it seemed to him that his happiness had come at last and was knocking.

And he told her about this, that he loved her and could not live without her.

In that very same instant her heart, flaming up, lit up only him, and he became for her the one being in the whole world, like an only child, more dear to her than Irinushka. She could not utter the words she wished to say; she could not utter that which was spoken so audibly by her heart, loving him once and for all time.

Then, in one instant, all that divided them became indivisible, and the impossible transformed itself into the possible, as wine becomes transformed into blood and bread into flesh.

Chapter V

A TIPSY crowd filed out noisily and unsteadily from the gay " New World." They
were putting out the lights in the " New World,"
were preparing to pass a stuffy night. The
musician was putting away his cheap music, the
pianist was striking his last hopeless note.

Once in the open, the master goldsmith, Semyon Mitrofanovitch, having thrown a thousand
aerial kisses toward the " New World," was
restless. He tore himself from Motya's embrace
and, clasping his arm around some one, an imaginary gay lady of some sort, tripped down the
street.

" That's how the cooperess tripped along with
the cooper,* heigh-ho, that was neither at home,
nor on the oven, hop along boots, jig along heels l
oho-ho . . ."—and, having exhausted himself,
the master goldsmith once more caught hold of
Motya—" Brother, I know a thing or two, and
take my word for it, the first thing to look to
is that the lady should hop along when she's
dancing, and she that hops along is a shrewd one
at things, you can't find a neater one. But you,
what do you understand ? Come, hand me a
match ! " He lit his pipe and spat. " Your
Raika** is a donkey, and you are an ass."

* The opening lines of a popular song.
** A contemptuous version of Raya's name.

148

" I understand everything," sniffed Motya.

" You understand nothing. As for me, old chap, I don't need any specs, and I'll open your eyes for you to everything. Yes, right now. Now tell me, have you earned much at the Klotchkovs'? Yes, much! You won't get a farthing. But as a fact, what old fool is going to pay you?"

" I'll have a talk with my sister Khristina."

" What have you got to say to her, you devil?"

" I'll talk to her about money, wages."

" Much good will it do you, you goose!"— and the master goldsmith pushed Motya.

Motya was roused.

" You're a goose yourself, a real tough."

By now the master goldsmith was in a boiling rage, and he shook his angry fists.

" I'll smash your jaw for you! You'd think he was King Mogol the great or other. You want to do him a favour and he's all in a huff —oh, you devil! If you like, I'll put some sense into your head. Come, what do you say?"

" Yes."

" Well, take my word for it. Get away from the Klotchkovs as soon as you can, and I shan't desert you, you may depend on that! Sanka tells me: ' I want you to come here! Senya!' she says, ' be sure to come and everything is ready, and you may bring your friend along too!' —Well, devil!"

"Khristina is no stranger to me. How will she manage it all by herself?"

"By herself?" burst out the master goldsmith. "By herself? And she with that grosbeak, Nelidov. . . . What's one to say after that? Are they any better than us?"

"Khristina is my sister."

"Sister! Sister, you say! Well, for my part, you can join the swine if you like!" The master goldsmith took a firm stride and, veering round sharply, caught Motya by the throat and pulled him gingerly about. "A drubbing would be too good for you, you drunkard. Tell me, you devil, you simpleton, what will become of you? Who's going to have a silly gander like you? To whom are you of any use, you friend of Shalyapin? A fine artist! A real wonder. . . . I want to make things easier for you—d'you understand?"

"I understand everything."

"You understand nothing!" The master goldsmith, releasing Motya, took him under the arm, and, as if nothing had happened, walked on peacefully, whispering the while: "Let's lose no time, brother. I will give the mistress notice, while you make a bolt for Petersburg with your Raika. If you let the moment go, you are lost. Sister! We know those sisters . . . the deuce take them!" Then he suddenly softened: "I tell you, Motya, honour bright, your sister is a first-class woman, and, of course, we are not educated ; we are only muzhiks ; we cannot, we belong to a rough folk . . . first class . . ."

And Semyon Mitrofanovitch fell into a gloomy mood, mumbled something quite incoherent, and complained, in the end giving way to abuse. He dragged Motya to the lamp-post and, unloading his heart upon the innocent iron, he bore his fellow-traveller along to the middle of the street. And he began to tell him about some strange uncatchable rats which had spread everywhere in all the houses and were eating up everything, but that in time the yard-men would drive out these rats with their brooms, and by then there would be no more muzhiks, no more rough folk, and they would all be given first-class things in order to enjoy life and to lose themselves in bliss. . . . And, kicking up the snow with his feet, the master goldsmith imitated a wild horse, and from a wild horse he changed quite suddenly into a jade fit for mourners at a funeral, and he trembled, mumbled, complained, and abused.

In Motya's oppressed head a single thought swung to and fro like a pendulum. He did not resist this thought, but tenaciously held on to it. He knew that if he tried to protest his foot would slip, he would fall into a snow-drift never to rise again. "He must without fail bolt from the Klotchkovs . . ."

" Seize the moment—seize the moment . . ." bellowed Motya.

The two friends at last managed to reach home.

And when the sleepy Ivan Trofimitch began to do his night duty, that of taking off the master goldsmith's boots, the gruff-tempered Semyon Mitrofanovitch suddenly beamed all over and, nudging a finger toward a dirty corner, where a dirty pail was put for the night, he said in a deliberate voice :

" Ivan, hand me that ! "

The boy bent over timidly and produced the desired pail.

" Pour yourself out a cup," ordered the master goldsmith, and opened his mouth wide with pleasure.

The boy poured himself out a cup of the nasty stuff, and, scenting what was coming, waited.

A long minute of painful waiting passed by.

" Lick it up ! " commanded the master goldsmith.

And the boy, making the sign of the cross over himself several times, drank the contents of the cup to the last drop.

Chapter VI

MOTYA snored. The master goldsmith snored.

The nose song resounded through the house with vigorous notes of whistling.

An impenetrable darkness hovered in the cold passage where lay Ivan Trofimitch shrinking within himself with loathing. He squirmed on his wretched little trunk, went on curling up his legs under his body until he resembled a pea ; then as he suddenly threw off his ragged cover, he violently shivered.

Now he shook with heat, now with cold ; the loathsome salt spittle stuck in his throat.

"Rotter . . ." whispered Ivan Trofimitch, "rotter. Oh, my dear mother, I pray you . . ."

On the other side of the wall lay Kostya, his head wrapped in his blanket ; he pressed against the wall to escape some one's horrible eyes, but these eyes, fixing him, drenched him in cold sweat.

Kostya dreamed of Katya. Katya appeared to ask him to go to a shop to buy her a coffin. And for a long time he walked among the shops and could not find a suitable coffin. But when he returned home he saw a coffin already there, and Katya standing near the coffin. Katya said to him : " Kostya, why did you buy me such a narrow, tight coffin?" And now they were lying side by side on a bed which sloped somewhat. Kostya was lying at the lower end, his hands touching the ground, and he felt it awkward and stifling and cold there; while Katya lay at the higher end, and she felt it good there, and soft and restful. Why did Katya feel it good, soft, and restful where she was, and why did he feel it awkward, stifling, and cold where he was? And why did he have a little star on his palm? And why was his nose crooked?

PART SIX

Chapter I

IT seemed at times to Nelidov that he had found in Khristina her whom he had lost for ever, her whom he had once loved—his betrothed. The dark nights flamed for him with a sun-like blaze. He took no heed of the hours, nor heard them strike: But one mood took possession of all objects and of his soul.

Yes, he had found in Khristina her whom he had lost for ever—his betrothed.

But the early, as yet dim, light looked into the window—the winter light just before daybreak—and he did not dare to look out of the window, and would have pierced his ears if he could but avoid listening to the beat of striking minutes. A kind of a monster crept out, as it were, from under the crumpled pillows, as yet warm with the night's caress, and crawled upon him with its slippery belly, pressed against his heart, tormented him, made game of him.

Why had he done it? He did not love Khristina. Why did he torment her? Why was he deceiving himself? Why did he pretend, if he knew that he did not love her? Why should he not tell the truth frankly, both to her and to himself? Or was he merely for-

getting ? How could he forget such a thing ?
"Consider," said the monster in a deliberate
fashion, "how she looks at you ! She believes
you and she loves you as you had loved your
betrothed—once and for ever, you will remember.
But soon she will scent the deception. And she
will become a disillusioned being. The world
will appear so small to her, and the sky so low,
and all the streets so narrow ; as you remember
everything appeared to you on that hot July midday, when you were returning from the graveyard, having lost for ever her whom you loved
so much—your betrothed. Yes, she will walk
in these narrow streets, and, recalling, her heart
will break and her bosom will droop. Soon ;
yes, soon, her scent will reveal to her your deception, and, confess it or not, it is all the same.
She will find out ; you cannot hide anything
from one who loves. You ought to know that,
you ought to bear that in mind, that is the truth.
You cannot hide anything from one who loves.
If not to-day, then to-morrow ; if not to-morrow,
then the day after to-morrow, everything shall
become known, without a single word being
said, but by means of the scent alone. She
thought that she had loved Sergey. She did not
love him, nor Sergey her. She does love you,
but you do not love her. Why do you deceive
her ? Why do you deceive yourself ?

All worn out, Nelidov tried to forget. But

not for long. The monster did not forsake him ; after a few moments it nudged him, pulled his covers off or grasped him by the shoulders, which trembled with a kind of ague.

Sometimes Nelidov jumped up out of bed and listened. It appeared to him that behind the wall some one was stealthily hammering a nail in, hammering it in strongly, as if it were meant to hold a noose, and for a head to slip into that noose. . . . As Nelidov listened a cold sweat appeared on his forehead and his teeth began to chatter. The despairing one on the other side of the wall must have managed it ; he must have put his head into the noose, given a kick with his feet, and it was done—he was hanging. A minute passed, another, a third. Nelidov made no stir, but listened and waited. And suddenly, so he thought, there was a growing clamour behind the wall : that meant they had found him, pulled the head of the unfortunate one from out of the noose, but too late.

"Too late," murmured Nelidov, "too late, he's beyond all help ! "—and he lay down again, and hoped to find a few moments' oblivion.

But somewhere from under the crumpled, as it were, molten hot pillows, the monster appeared to creep out once more, and to throw itself upon him with its slippery belly, to press against his heart, to torment him, to make game of him.

Why had he done it? He did not love Khristina. Why did he torment her? Why was he deceiving himself? Why did he pretend, if he knew that he did not love her? Why should he not tell the truth frankly, both to her and to himself? Or was he merely forgetting? How could he forget such a thing?

The day came and went in sluggish confusion. Then the evening came. Khristina usually called in the evening, or he went to the Klotchkovs.

When he was with her he forgot everything. He simply could not understand how the thought could have come into his head that he was deceiving her, or that he was deceiving himself. After all, he was quite sincere when he had said to himself that he loved her, and that he could not live without her. Yes, he was quite sincere; he had deceived no one.

In that way, going against himself, against his deepest consciousness, Nelidov did everything to hide the truth from himself, but reaching the highest point of his torture, in the very heat of his effort at self-consolation, his heart would suddenly sink within him and his whole being would give itself up to listening; that voice, which hid itself by day and crept out, a monster, before dawn, caught the reproaches as in a sharp net, and, like a king and judge, imperiously pronounced upon him: "*Condemned to death!*"

And he saw in all objects and in all eyes a

silent assent to the sentence : " Condemned to death ! "

And she, Death, the intractable, whom he, in vain, had called twice from the depth of his heart, could not help but appear, could not help but answer the call, could not help but receive him.

And having a sense of this, he—a certain Mr. Nelidov, one of a thousand from which he differed in name only, a former official, actor, and schoolmaster, caught in the whirlpool of all sorts of pettiness and fretfulness, merely to go on living —now, for the first time, found strength in his heart to meet her boldly.

Before Shrovetide there was a fair in town. The shops closed late, and Khristina could not go to Nelidov, and he did not call on the Klotch-kovs.

He did not want to see Khristina ; there was no need for him to see her on the eve of his last day.

Chapter II

ON the eve of that same day the master goldsmith, Semyon Mitrofanovitch, left the Klotchkovs.

That was the first blow which came down on Khristina, after which there showered down upon her, like nuts, all sorts of misfortunes. She never thought for a moment that all things would come down at once like that. And there fell upon her that unconcern which faithfully foreboded a bitter to-morrow.

Kostya alone, suddenly becoming silent, dozed behind the counter, and muttered all sorts of nonsense in his sleep, then waking, he walked about gloomily, biting his lip, as if he were preparing for some great, unheard-of affair.

On Saturday, after dinner, a process-server appeared at the Klotchkovs' to seize the shop.

The process-server put a chain on the door, read his official paper, placed two constables at the door, and proceeded with his business.

Khristina, Motya, Raya, and Ivan Trofimitch stood behind the counter in a straight line, and their faces appeared quite business-like, as if nothing unusual had happened and everything was in order ; and only in the eyes of each, as yet unnoticed by them, there lurked one turning thought about to-morrow : what would they do to-morrow ?

Kostya, immersed in his all-absorbing thought of accomplishing some unheard-of deed, stood rather away from the rest, blew out his cheeks and played furiously with his tongue.

Passers-by paused at the windows, looked in, stuck their tongues out, showed their teeth, made faces ; they could not repress the peculiar joy awakened in them by a neighbour's misfortune. Of course, it was not a thing to poke into one's eyes, for no one can say what will happen to anyone else—we are all subject to God's will, but it was hard to repress oneself. And the process-server, as he put the seals on the costly things and gew-gaws, barely restrained a smile.

As for the clocks, they went on as before ; they were the same before the seizure and after it. Some of them cried out their slender worn-out song, of the emptiness of life with its dull decorum, its respectable restraint and its timorous falsehood. Others, with a prolonged hollow sound, struck the hour of death, arousing fear in people, who had been deceived by the slender, worn-out song, that of the pettiness of life.

And the gramophone rattled on a prancing, audacious dance, shamelessly, without restraint, and shook in a shivering way.

" That's how the cooperess tripped along with

the cooper ! "* said the process-server, unable to resist any longer, with a snap of his fingers.

The process-server was putting on the seals, one after another, on all the walls and on all the show-cases, stopping up the throats of all the objects.

The shop was expiring.

When the seizure was completed and the process-server departed, only a few small time-pieces, left unsealed by chance, ticked faintly, and their ticking was such as gave one the feeling of slender little nails passing over one's heart, catching it with their points and delicately tearing it.

So it appeared to Khristina, and she made haste to leave by the back door of the sealed-up dead shop, no longer her own.

Raya and Motya exchanged glances : everything had already been arranged between them. Raya and Motya only waited for the evening : in the evening they would take their seats in the train and make straight for St. Petersburg to their friend Senya—the master goldsmith, Semyon Mitrofanovitch—and start their new life.

" Forgive and farewell, don't bear us a grudge !" sang Motya, twisting his little moustaches and distending his nostrils, as if he were Shalyapin, or Shalyapin's friend.

Ivan Trofimitch, crushed under his fur cap,

* See footnote, page 148.

was returning home, to his dark little corridor, slowly and gloomily, as if he bore fifty years on his back. Where could he go, where was he to start his new life ?

" I'll join the fire department," mused Ivan Trofimitch dejectedly. " I'll risk my skin. . . . I wonder how I shall ever manage the helmet, all brass, at least a ton ! Or else I'll join a band of robbers, announce freedom to everybody, and Semyon Mitrofanovitch . . . I'll . . . with an axe . . ."

Chapter III

FOR the last time Kostya was ascending the cathedral belfry to wind up the clock. He leaped upward from step to step as in a single breath.

And the wind, coming on, struck him hard on his chest, tried to hurl him below.

"You dare not ! You dare not !" the wind, so it seemed to Kostya, shouted at him through the apertures.

And the hoary bells trembled, tried to frighten him ; they droned their eternal drone, and, droning, they threatened, with their cast-iron tongues, to shatter the skull of the big-nosed monster, who had conceived an unheard-of deed.

Kostya felt no fatigue. He knew no fear. What were fatigue and fear to him ? His heart was being consumed in one hard, irrevocable desire ; he had thought out a thought yet greater than all thoughts.

It was neither man nor wild beast, but Time with his hours who ruled over life and sent it days and nights ; everything came from him— all the torments and sufferings of life. And he would kill Time—the accursed one !—he would kill him with his hours and he would free himself, the whole earth, and the whole universe. There on the earth his feet would be no longer,

and he would not descend from the belfry before
he had accomplished his deed. If need be,
he would climb even higher, upon the cupola
itself ; he would rise upon the cross and even
higher . . . he was ready to climb upon the
clouds. He had sworn and would swear by all
the days of his crooked-nosed misery, by his
hopeless love for Lydotchka Lisitsina ; he had
sworn by the sun and the night—the sun, by
the light of which they tormented him ; the
night, under whose roof he, all worn out, had
devised his infliction.

" Kostya, if only there were no clocks at all,
then time would not exist, neither the present,
nor the past, nor the future ! " flared up for an
instant Nelidov's words, spoken a month ago,
and they gave Kostya still further assurance.

Having reached the topmost landing, Kostya,
with a strange ease, managed everything in connection with the winding up of the clock, which
had yielded to him before with the greatest
difficulty.

The winding lever turned like a thin straw in
his hands.

Kostya listened ; the clock seethed with life,
swarmed as with a thousand thousand scurrying
years, a thousand thousand small poisonous
worms. And upon this iron monstrosity
depended his fate, as well as the fate of the earth
and of the whole universe. No, he could no

longer live, nor walk upon the earth, without first casting off the iron yoke ; with his own hands he would throttle this iron throat !

His mouth slightly open, his half-battered teeth tightly clenched, Kostya caught hold of an iron rod. And pushing it forward as if it were no more than a feather, he swung toward the window opening, clambered deftly on to the sill, bent himself in two, and, reaching out his hand in a superhuman way, he touched the big hand of the clock with the obedient iron rod, hooked it and led it forward. He led it slowly, and put the clock a whole hour forward—from a quarter-past to half-past, from half-past to a quarter to, from a quarter to to ten minutes to, from ten to to five to, from five to to three to, then to a minute to. . . . And pausing to take an instant's breath, he tore with the iron rod at the big hand.

The broken clock-hand gave a crackle, then a tinkle, and, glimmering with a small blue flame, was lost in the starry night.

And the clock bell swung its cast-iron tongue in its singing heart and began to sing its ancient, immutable song—the bell struck its hour.

The clock could not stay its appointed strokes. Ten strokes rolled by, one after another—nine appointed by God, the tenth by Kostya.

Terror and wailing and laughter tore themselves from the singing heart of the bell.

The waning tones, rising from the earth, flew

toward the stars and, dissipating into a transparent white vapour, wavered like white feathers. . . .

And the blue stars were thinking their distant starry thoughts and sparkled in the shelter of their light.

A painful quiet settled upon the earth.

The town, living according to the cathedral clock, gave a start.

A fireman in the watch-tower, wrapped in his sheepskin, his terrible bronze helmet on his head, paused suddenly and began to look for the fire ; but the red glow above the belfry died out, and the fireman once more began to pace round the four dark signal-balls and ringing wires. The departing trains, an hour late, speeded up under increased steam, and whistled desperately. Hungry, jaded horses were lashed on by the cabbies, themselves under the whip of belated, nervous passengers, hurrying to keep their appointments. A telegraph operator, bent into a harness arch, made his exhausted finger dance even more briskly across the keys of his instrument, breaking off messages and sending across all sorts of nonsense and cock-and-bull stories. Young *ladies* from the gay " New World " were roused from their unfinished sleep, and, in expectation of guests, smeared white paint across their spotted blue cheeks and the ineradicable ulcers upon their worn crumpled breasts. The notary, glad of the hour, and finishing his business for the day, was putting into his portfolio a pile of lapsed bills for protest. The graveyard watchman, a spade under his arm, was on his way to dig graves for to-morrow's corpses. The publican was opening up his last bottles. And the government dram-shop was being closed. Misery and sorrow and all their sisters passed through the town gate, scattered themselves throughout the town, entered the houses of the fated ones. And the marked soul was agitated. As he looked with his senseless eyes somewhere upon the dimmed full moon, tipsy in the cloud-haze, the crazed Markusha-*Napoleon* delightedly uttered his night prayer : " O Lord, cast upon us Thy light of the sun, the moon, and the stars ! "

Having fallen backward on the stone landing and not having heard the clock bell, Kostya came to his senses again, and, jumping on to the sill like a cat, looked at the clock.

One single small hand rested motionlessly on the clock.

At last Kostya's hour had come ! Kostya had killed accursed time !

There was no more the irrevocable. There was no more expectation. There was no more time !

And, stretching his neck forward in goose-like fashion, resting his bony hands on the stone window-sill, Kostya burst into a full-throated, mad, wild laughter.

THE CLOCK

Kostya's hour had come ! Kostya had killed accursed time !

There was no more the irrevocable. There was no more expectation. There was no more time !

And, having thrown a kiss to the crowded town which he had freed, he began to sing a kingly song of a deliverer.

Kostya sang, Kostya Klotchkov, a king, who had attended to time with its anguish and bereavement, a king of kings, a deliverer of the earth and of the universe from the iron yoke of the hours.

There was no more the irrevocable. There was no more expectation. There was no more time.

Chapter IV

KOSTYA'S small, hunched figure, looking in its hood very much like a hare, hopped peacefully along the river and darted out of the snowdrifts.

Kostya paused before the governor's house and glanced through the gates.

" It's too much trouble to tell him ; let him find out for himself ! " decided Kostya about the governor, on whom he had meant to call in order to announce a free new life without time. He walked on farther.

As he came up to the sentry's hut, he shouted to the sentry :

" I never saw the governor's wife. They say she's an old woman, but very charming."

There was a bonfire in the square, and a policeman and some vagrants had gathered round it.

One of the vagrants said :

" There won't be any more time."

Kostya nodded his head as a mark of his favour.

" You are right, there won't be any more time. It is I who have made you folk free, I—Kostya Klotchkov ; from now on everything is possible, and there is no impossible ! " And he walked on farther.

Thus Kostya went on, saying encouraging

words to his freed slaves—his subjects, without observing the time.

The house porters were shutting the gates for the night. Evil dogs were being let loose in the yards. Homeless beings were already beginning to appear in the streets ; they lurked stealthily along the walls, within wall gates, and they jumped and shivered with the cold.

On a bench near a grimy lodging-house sat two little beggar-women, and, as if nothing had happened, were abusing things and exchanging beggars' gossip.

Kostya interrupted them :

" Why are you sitting there, little beggar-women ? Haven't you heard ? There isn't any more time, and everything is done and there is nothing to argue about ! "—and, drawing from his pocket the key of the clock, he threw it in their faces. " Here, take this planet meat and distribute it among the poor ; I don't want any-one to complain. From now on everything is possible, and there is no impossible ! "

At that moment, as if risen from the earth, Nelidov appeared ; he was on his way to the railway station. Kostya knew him at once by his high hat.

" Where are you off to, Mr. Nelidov ? " asked Kostya, and made him stop.

Nelidov took out his watch, glanced at it, and said :

THE CLOCK

"I have but a half-hour left, Kostya. Good-bye!"

"One would think he was condemned to death!" exclaimed Kostya, enraged and startled at this unyielding attitude of Nelidov, who had dared to speak of time; but remembering that time had been crushed by him for ever, and that things could no longer be the same, he went off into a frenzied twirl.

And Kostya twirled round and round, down the street, like a merry-go-round at a Shrovetide fair.

He imagined that he himself was a merry-go-round, upon which anyone could ride without paying.

A number of ragged urchins, pouring out into the night from their holes and lodgings to pursue their petty thievery, threw themselves toward Kostya, and, surrounding him from all sides, twirled round with him like merry-go-rounds.

Kostya regarded the urchins with approval; he promised to show them the show-tents, in which kings and grandees would play Punch and Judy, and he, a great clown, first and last, would fell the sun for laughter; because from now on, when time had ceased to be, everything was possible, and there was no impossible.

"Tooy-tooy-rata-tooy!" gasped Kostya, and went on twirling like a merry-go-round.

And as he went on twirling, Kostya began to

feel as if something were slowly but stubbornly thawing somewhere in his heart, and an enormous wall almost unnoticeably but surely leaning over him, while the growing consciousness of a fabulous strength, of a boundless might, urged him to twirl like a merry-go-round.

" You slabbering kids, I give you a freedom, such as no nation has yet had since the creation of the world and love and death.   Listen to me, you ragamuffins and thieves : I have seized Time, and I have killed him and all his hours—from now on there is no time !   Listen to me, you good-for-nothings : I have taken to me the sin of the world ; I have killed sin with all his sadness and despair—from now on there is no more sin ! Listen to me, cowards and cheats : I have taken to me death ; I have killed death and all her terror —from now on there is no death !   From now on there is no time ; from now on everything is possible, and there is no impossible.   And I give to you, who are hungry and weary, the best of everything, so that you may enjoy yourselves and wallow in bliss !   Enjoy yourselves in plenty, happy slaves, rakes and libertines, my own dear brothers, for whom it is my will to cut up chunks of meat and to stuff up your own gluttonous, greedy gullets.   I am the Lord your God ! "

One of the ragamuffins from among the *tom-cats* struck Kostya's cap off, and jeered at him as he spat into his face !

THE CLOCK

" And what will I get, Kostya ? "

" You will lick my small pig," said Kostya, as he good-naturedly wiped his face, and, turning to the collected Shrovetide crowd, he cried out : " Come to me ! " Then he smiled : " I am something of a crow ! "

Still smiling, he went on farther.

Kostya walked on, taking no notice of the time, and with a finger cut circles in the air round his nose.

He had enough of lounging about ; a ravenous *wasp-eater*, by day he would manage things according to his own inclination ; he would beat his prey until its blood had become froth ; while at night, having filled all the wells with frog spawn, he would follow an occupation : hounding little children to death . . . he would drown the little blind ones in nice warm water, so they should not feel cold.

" The old man went—did not reach the place, the young man went—could not find it,* the devil is glad," said Kostya with a smile, put his hands into his pockets and, imagining himself a frog's leg, perched his lantern on his shoulder.

The lantern lurched forward and dashed against the pavement ; there was a crash of glass.

Kostya tore himself away from the place and began to run. He ran like a horse. He was

* Popular Russian adage.

neither a merry-go-round, nor a Punch and Judy, nor a wasp-eater, nor a frog's foot; he was a horse, a grey horse, a dapple-grey horse, with silver saddle, and a gilt bridle. He would gallop to the cathedral, buy up all the church candles, he would sit down at the high altar, he would wash himself in the cold dew, he would read all the books, and he would kindle like a three-hundred-pound candle before Palm-Sunday, in front of Lydotchka Lisitsina. He had on a silken girdle, a beaver cap, an overcoat of satin and fur, and his nose was as in a picture. He was no longer Kostya Klotchkov, but the instructor and detective Kourinas, the first and the last, Kourinas Kourinasovitch. A black-limbed horse, he strikes the ground with his hoofs, and lays such enormous eggs in the sand, both goose and duck eggs.

"Cluck-cluck-cluck! a goose and a duck!" shouted Kostya at the top of his voice down the street, and, scattering right and left the golden nuts he had obtained somewhere, he imagined himself to be standing at the door of the Lisitsins' trinket-shop, and left as if something, lit with a match, blazed into a green little flame, and painfully went round and round in his brain.

"Oh, you speckled, puffed-up hens!" shouted Kostya, as he pulled at the door of the trinket-shop, and, throwing open his uncommon overcoat of poppy-flower leaf, he intently fixed his eyes upon Lydotchka.

Lydotchka, struck dumb with fright, could only gape with her pretty azure-blue eyes, and, without uttering a sound, fell back in her seat.

Kostya, biting a whitened lip and trembling all over, crept stealthily towards the counter. He advanced a foot with the intention of jumping over the counter, but for some reason reconsidered. Instead, he bent over it, clutched at the frightened girl, and pulled her across the counter ; then, pressing her to him, he fastened his lips upon hers and kissed her sugary lips and her rosy cheeks, with a violence, noisy and smack-resounding ; then, suddenly, he opened his mouth wide, and clutch !—he made dessert of her sugary-shaped porcelain little nose. . . .

Lydotchka groaned, closed her pretty azure-blue eyes, and fainted away. Lydotchka became quite helpless, like a corpse ; she no longer resisted the terrible Kostya's terrible embraces and kisses.

The commotion brought out the sandy-haired shop assistant, *Little Wise Head*, who, shaking his bald-growing pate, and swearing for all he was worth, caught hold of Kostya, and, pulling him away from the mangled Lydotchka, threw him through the door into the street as if he were a cat.

THE CLOCK

Kostya's flight ended in the snow, and he heard the door of the shop bang.

Through his tears his trembling lips hummed a nursery song, which he had heard Khristina sing over her Irinushka, and a kind of deathly terror, springing to his heart, lifted him up from the earth.

Kostya rose and went down the street, staggering, no longer Kostya Klotchkov, or a merry-go-round, or a Punch and Judy, or a wasp-eater, or a frog's leg, or the instructor and detective Kourinas, or a black-limbed horse, but a humiliated *donkey* on a black-beetle's legs.

People darted all around him, ran after him, but did not touch him nor jostle him, a humiliated donkey on a black-beetle's legs.

The carnival street dinned with hundreds of drunken voices. And each voice flew into Kostya's ear, so that it appeared to Kostya that he was all-hearing.

The carnival street dinned.

" I wanted to ask you how our affair is progressing ! " some one's voice pierced Kostya's all-hearing ear.

Some one else was saying quite another thing :

" The devil, you ought to have a wet rag put on your nose ! "

A third was addressing a fourth :

" Give me a light ! Old chap, do give me a light ! "

"Ooh ! What a fool !" snapped the fourth.

A twentieth, rather hoarse voice apologized :

"I haven't a farthing on me. I'm sorry !"

"Must I tell you again that I've lost my matches ?" growled a hundredth.

But the hundred-and-first was interrupting him.

"Chuck him, but look well about you !" insisted the two-hundred-and-first.

And, without any apparent connection, a thousand-and-third was arguing :

"While another fool works all his life, how's one to understand ?"

"I wonder why my man hasn't turned up yet ?" complained a woman's tipsy voice.

An elderly voice began to sing with a shrill wail :

"A you-th lu-u-res a mai-den . . ."

Then a despairing voice :

"There is no answer, not one good word."

Some one was trying to quiet an old woman :

"Aren't you ashamed of yourself—so old and to sing songs ?"

And some one said threateningly :

"Now, don't fool with me, or you'll get something !"

And some one was abusive :

"May the devil take you !"

And a policeman's slender tenor sang out, accompanied by the clapping of hands :

" That's the way the cooperess tripped along with her cooper ! "*

The hundreds of drunken holiday voices went on dinning and dinning.

" But what do they want ? " Kostya asked himself. " I gave them planet meat, I gave them everything. . . . And what can I want now, to be a king over kings ? "

In the sealed-up Klotchkov shop, no longer lit up by the little lamp-guardian, there was visible through the window grating something dark, like an eye-hole.

At the window of the shop stood Khristina, thinking of something.

Kostya, on seeing Khristina, ran to her.

And they stood looking at one another : he a preying *wasp-eater*, she a dove. And he pierced her from head to foot with his senseless glance of a wasp-eater.

" Kostya, what is the matter with you, Kostya ? " said Khristina, very much frightened.

At that moment some one on the pavement cried threateningly :

" Hey, Kostya, what do you mean by wearing your cap like that ? I'll teach you something later ! "

Kostya heard the threat and was silent, and silently he pierced Khristina with his senseless glance of a wasp-eater.

* See footnote, page 148.

He was a wasp-eater, she a dove.

" You are ill, Kostya.   Go home, Kostya ! "—
and tears appeared in Khristina's eyes.

And again something, as if struck with a
match, blazed into a small green flame, and painfully began to go round and round, in Kostya's
sick brain, and the enormous wall had quite
come down on him.

Kostya stretched out both his hands toward
Khristina, and, looking close into her face, said
in a whisper :

" I feel a pain, Khristina, a great pain ; but if
anyone should ask you, Khristina, as to what
Kostya had said, tell them that Kostya had said,
' *Nitzchevo* ! '*—and, putting out his tongue,
Kostya went his way.

Gloom settled on Kostya's soul, a gnawing
sadness seized him.

" Oh, stars, take me ! " was the last cry which
tore itself from his heart, worn out with torture.

As if in answer to this cry of a tortured heart,
the light for a moment died in his eyes, and then
some one on slender womanish legs—so it seemed
to Kostya—someone altogether thin, quiet, transparent, like a net, indeed, Kostya's own devil,
appeared on the pavement scurrying on his little
feet.

The devil pursued Kostya ; now he disappeared,
then again reappeared, and with his laughing,

* " Nothing ! " or, " Never mind ! "

big-nosed face looked many times straight into Kostya's eyes.

" Kostya, great Kostya, saviour of the human race, deliverer of the world from the iron yoke "—the Big-nosed one trembled—" you are a god, a king, a king over kings ; you have conquered time, you have given freedom to humanity, all lands are subject to you, everything under the moon, the whole world. Kostya, you are not Kostya, you are not Kostya Klotchkov ; you are Kostya Sabaoth. You have but to wish it and the stars would fall from the sky, and the sun would go out ; but all the same, Kostya, dear Kostya, dear little unfortunate Kostya, you have a crooked nose ! "

And suddenly, with an agile movement, the Big-nosed one caught Kostya under an arm—so it appeared to Kostya—and led him away, crossing many bridges toward Kostya's new palace and temple and skies.

And Kostya saw clearly how in the starry skies three black columns erected themselves, and upon the black columns sat three green priests, erect ; the priests read three red books.

Kostya was not astonished, and he did not resist the Big-nosed one. Kostya hopped along with the Big-nosed one, not Kostya Klotchkov, but Kostya Sabaoth, and he stuck out his tongue and smiled. He looked round him with his godly eyes. What else should he, the almighty

Kostya, devise ? What other worlds, lands, should he create ? . . . Or should he transform all the angels into devils ; or put a clock-glass across the sky, so that the happenings in the skies may be visible and that the skies should not get dusty ? Or should he mix everything up, confuse the whole appearance of the world, and rest as on the seventh uncreative day, not as a pigeon, but as a crow ?

" What a crow I am ! " mumbled Kostya, smiling, and, sticking out his tongue, he followed his way, approaching every moment nearer his new palace, temple, and skies, his kingdom of madness.

Chapter V

KHRISTINA could hardly bear up on her legs. Wishing to save if only a little, she walked across the whole town, from one end to the other. But she had no luck : either the door was slammed in her face, or it was too late, or she was simply not received.

"It looks as if no one will have anything to do with me," she thought, and lost heart.

And when at last, all worn out, Khristina returned home and looked for Motya, neither Motya nor Raya was at home ; their tracks had cooled long ago.

"Both he and the young lady have left the house," said the reticent Frosya, in whose ears hung ear-rings of incredible proportions, given to her by Motya ; then she burst out sobbing— "He's quite a dashing fellow, your brother, Matvey Mikhailovitch. May God forgive them ! "

A foreboding of some greater misfortune took hold of Khristina. Could she have cried, she would have felt easier, but no tears would come ; burning, they poured themselves out somewhere in the depth of her heart. She felt as if a pair of arms had lifted her up from the earth and held her over an abyss. And the words choked in her tightened throat ; it was hard for her to utter a single word.

THE CLOCK

She ran her eyes over a letter she had just received from Sergey. Sergey wrote her that he could no longer go on living as he did, that only now he had begun to realise how much he loved her, and that he had finally decided to return and would be home the day after to-morrow.

"He'll arrive to-morrow . . ." reflected Khristina ; " he has begun to realize his love ; but then . . . *if you love, but are not loved in return, you are lost.* . . ." And remembering Nelidov, she suddenly asked herself : " But does he love me ? If he loves me, why is he not here ? And he was not here yesterday. Why hasn't he come either yesterday or to-day ? "

Khristina decided to see Nelidov at once.

She would ask him why he hasn't come either yesterday or to-day ; she would tell him all her suspicions, all her thoughts, all her doubts. It was hard for her, all alone like that. But she was not to blame. She would entreat him to tell her the truth, the most horrible truth—she would face it, she was afraid of nothing, only he must tell her the truth : did he love her or not ? . . . To-morrow Sergey would arrive. She had a child, and everything had been seized. She had nothing. How was she to live ? Why hasn't he come, why ? If but for a minute, to inquire how things were going. The whole town knew that the shop had been seized. Why hadn't he called yesterday ? But if he loved her . . .

184

Didn't he love her ? . . . Well, let him tell the truth ; he must tell her, he must tell her the whole truth.

Nelidov's house was shut. She had to go to the office. And in the office they told her that he had left town.

" He has left town for good ; he has gone to his native village," said the house porter.

Her thoughts got into a tangle.

" How could that be ? Without letting her know ? Without a word ? What native village ? Where was his native village ? "

And a black shadow fell upon her soul.

Khristina felt this shadow, and she knew that she would never come out from under it.

" If you love, and are not loved in return, you are lost. . . ." No, not that . . . to love and not to wish to possess one's beloved—is impossible ; but to possess a person and to destroy him, it's all one in the end. No, that's not it . . ." were the thoughts and words which glimmered in her mind.

But she had no time to reflect ; she did everything on the spur of the moment.

Khristina stopped a cabby and ordered him to drive to the station.

What would Nelidov tell her now ? What could he tell her ?

" And if it should be asked what Kostya had said, tell them that Kostya had said, '*Nitzchevo!*'"

rang Kostya's last words suddenly in her ears.

But perhaps all this was only a dream, and she would soon awake?

"O Lord, if it were only all a dream—*nitz-chevo!*"

"Why is the big clock-hand gone?" asked Khristina of the cabby, as they passed by the cathedral belfry.

"We know nothing," replied the old cabby; "it may so please God."

"It may so please God . . ." repeated Khristina, and she repeated the words with all her heart and soul, and forgot all about the clock-hand and what she had asked the cabby.

What God? And why did it please Him so? What was her suffering to Him? Did she not pray to Him? Did she not entreat Him to help her? She had prayed to Him so passionately. She had believed and hoped so strongly. And what of Him? Why did it please Him so? What was her suffering to Him? Where was He to be found? Did he hear her? If He heard her, how could He let all that happen, for she had prayed to Him? . . . Why, then, should she pray? One may as well not pray. . . .

"O Lord! O Lord! I believe. You shall hear me. You are all-powerful. You shall hear me! You see everything. Forgive! My whole life is before You, and I have no one and I come to You, as to my last shelter. I am alone. You can see. I am alone. Help me !"

Khristina got out of the cab and walked on foot the rest of the way. She walked rapidly, as if she were gliding on skates, and observed nothing about her.

She found herself at the railway station.

The station was packed with people.

She hunted among the tables, jostling her way past people, and looked for Nelidov high and low. She thought she saw a glimmer of his high hat above other heads.

" He's here ; he's not left yet," she thought, and resumed her search.

But no, she was mistaken ; he was no longer here.

Khristina hurried out on the platform.

There were many people waiting for the train. It was said that the train was late, but would soon arrive.

" That means the train has not left yet ! " thought Khristina joyfully, and walked up and down the station about ten times, scrutinizing every face.

No, she was mistaken ; he was no longer here.

" Perhaps he was somewhere there behind the train carriages, waiting for her ! "—and she descended on the tracks and walked along the side-path.

Khristina walked past the signals and the switchman's hut and crossed the bridge, then walked on past vacant lots and kitchen-gardens.

Above the little wood, where the tracks took a turn, a star shone brightly, as if it shone for her and led her along the path beyond the vacant lots and the kitchen-gardens.

And suddenly Khristina heard, somewhere afar, the ring of the bell—the first, the second, the third. . . . And at that same moment a bright light lit up the road-bed, and, increasing in intensity, travelled along the now sounding rails.

And it seemed to her as if the star, flaring up, was rapping over the trees of the little wood. Like death, a thing of terror, the train was bearing down upon Khristina.

" Oh Lord ! " cried Khristina, and leapt aside from the rails ; something in her heart tore and snapped.

She saw flying in front of the speeding train, lit up by the reflectors, a man in a high hat ; it was Nelidov flying with outspread arms, like a huge black eagle. She saw him flying a long time, a black eagle ; then fell his unfaithful wings, and he fell face foremost upon a sleeper.

And the hissing steel paws caught up their prey and, breathing fire, and whistling, rent it into many small pieces.

The train dashed on, faster and faster, greased with thick human blood.

And there, over the little wood, the star went on rapping.

Chapter VI

IT was long past midnight.

Behind the cold samovar, in her usual place, sat Khristina like one taken down from the cross. She had been sitting like this a long time, from the hour when she was brought from the station barely alive. A stubborn, pressing thought contracted her forehead into a deep, old-womanish wrinkle.

The old man, bulging his eyes, was reclining on the sofa ; and it appeared to the old man that his head was overlaid with black-beetles' eggs. It also appeared to him that he was surrounded by horrible faces with red beards ; one small devilkin, his back bent into a ring, was filing one of his feet, while another pug-nosed one was applying a red-hot iron to the sole.

"There is no pity anywhere ! There is no one to go to ! There is no pity anywhere !" groaned the old man helplessly, tormented with pain.

And the horrible faces with the red beards vanished for a moment as if they wished to grant him a respite, but, having cunningly given him hope, they reappeared. They shook their red beards, performed agile antics on the floor, made thrusts at the old man ; one small devilkin, his back bent into a ring, was filing one of his feet, another pug-nosed one was applying a red-hot iron to the sole.

"There is no pity anywhere! There is no one to go to!" There is no pity anywhere!" groaned the old man helplessly, tormented with pain.

The lamp on the table, burning itself out, was flickering.

The night with open mouth blew on the dying flame, and nimble shadows darted round like mice and leapt upon the darkening face of the old man, round his bristly grey eyebrows, and, contracting, crept across the beard into his open mouth.

And dark and inexorable, they crept—these dark nocturnal shadows—upon the floor, upon the carpet, upon the table, upon Khristina, upon the table, upon the floor, upon the carpet, in all corners, through the whole Klotchkov house.

And, sleepless, they lay down to sleep their dog-like slumber.

The Klotchkov dog Koupon, tossing at the feet of the old man, dreamt that he was not a house-dog, but a yard-dog—a watch-dog—and that he had a warm kennel, and that some one came and for no reason docked his tail and ruined his kennel.

Koupon went on tossing restlessly at the old man's feet.

And only in the store-room, between the doors, whither he retired late that evening, there sat upon a slop-pail, as upon a throne, Kostya himself—not Kostya Klotchkov, but Kostya Sabaoth ; not Kostya Sabaoth, but a crow ; and he sat there as if time did not exist ; happy and contented ; he laid goose eggs and duck eggs, counted black-beetles' skins, in order to save others from counting the accursed skins in the future, and he picked at his deformed nose, with zeal and enjoyment.

But the time went on, the clock ticked off instant after instant, into an abyss from which there is no return, repeating one and the same thing, as yesterday, so to-day also.

The clock in the cathedral belfry struck three.

There rolled by, one after the other, three prolonged, pensive strokes, three fore-ordained ancient chimes.

And it was deathly still upon the earth.

The waning tones, rising upon the earth, flew toward the stars, and, dissipating into a transparent white vapour, wavered like white feathers.

And the distant blue stars sang their last supramundane songs ; unearthly, yet they covered the cold sky with an earthly sadness.

"Stop your pranks, Kostya ! " cried the old cathedral watchman ·in his sleep, and, thrusting his head upward, he suddenly bent low again and began morosely to pace his beat round the cold, austere and proud, white-stoned belfry.

High above the houses, at the topmost tier of the cathedral belfry, in the window opening, leaning his bony palms on the stone window-sill, and stretching his neck forward like a goose, some one was pouring out his laughter, his wrinkled grey eyes welling with tears, and through his laughter and his tears he sent kisses down to the earth in that starry night.

THE END.

A White Heart

A WHITE HEART

A Contemporary Legend

I WAS waiting for a tram-car. There was no way of getting on ; people were hanging on, jostling one another. Well, simply like wild beasts. Ten tram-cars I let go past. I saw an old woman standing there, like myself, waiting. An ancient grandmother. To look at her face you would have thought that it had always been like that, that she had always been a grandmother ; her wrinkles were so minute ; she was toothless, and goodness was in her face. I looked more intently ; she was standing patiently. Did her tired eyes see anything ? Yes, they saw.

"Don't leave me to myself," said to me the grandmother. "Let us go on the tram together. I simply can't manage to crowd in."

"All right," said I. "We'll go together. Only we'll have to wait here for some time. I'm no good for pushing, or hanging on."

"God preserve us from that !" the grandmother interrupted me.

Yes, the grandmother saw that she was not alone.

A young woman was standing near us, and it was quite clear that she was with us ; but the young woman could hold out no longer, and when the eleventh tram came up she suddenly changed —what had become of her gentleness ! She joined the tram crowd and hung on with the rest.

The matter had become desperate for us. Nothing seemed left for us to do but to go on foot.

" Let us go, grandmother ; it's all the same."

" I'll never get so far."

It was true. The old woman could have never got there. We were standing on a corner of the 9th Line, and the grandmother's destination was the New Village.

I conquered my despair, and it was evident that the grandmother had conquered hers long ago. At last, with God's help, we got a tram and pushed in.

The tram was full ; it was useless even to think of a seat. They were all soldiers. As for me, I'm no good at hanging on ; still, I managed to stand somehow. It was different with the old woman ; she bent quite in two, and her legs refused to obey her—she was like a blade of grass at every jolt.

" Won't some one give grandmother a seat ? " said I to the passengers.

This was not the first time I had spoken like that, so I did not expect any mercy. But this time it seemed to work : two sailors rose from their seats.

" There are good people in this world—please sit down."

I seated the grandmother.

It is good for a man to be like these sailors. I looked at them, and perhaps, even standing they felt at that instant as happy as the grandmother.

As for her, having rested a while, she began to talk. Though she did not speak loudly, every word of hers was audible ; there was something in her voice which cheered even the sailors, who had given up their place to her ; her harshest words came from a white heart.

The old grandmother told about herself, of the place she had come from, and of her hard and lonely life. And in the course of her story she recalled the present, as it were, and, raising her eyes to me, repeated :

" Don't leave me to myself. We'll get off together."

" Together ! Together, grandmother ! " repeated I, as well as the two sailors, rocking from the jolts. Without words, they seemed to say as they rocked : " Together, together ! "

It was hard for the grandmother in the white world ; that was the word she used—" hard." The grandmother was not a native here ; her own country was at the other end of the world, somewhere near Kovno. Many times she had been driven out ; they always told her that the

Germans were coming. Nothing was certain for some time ; she would gather up her goods and get ready to go ; then one day would pass, then another, and everything would be as it was before, and she would remain.

"In the end they made it hard for me, and I had to go."

"Who made it hard for you—the Germans ?"

"No !" said the grandmother, as she remembered something very bitter, but she added, in a voice without bitterness : "*My own children*."

The soldier passengers exchanged glances. And the voice of the old woman became even more audible. For some reason the whole car grew quiet, and no one went out. Did they all go the same way—grandmother's way ?

"I had a little house. I thought I'd die there. I was quite alone in the white world. I had had a daughter of about sixteen ; she died. Another daughter married, lived a year and died. I had three sons, who worked in a factory here in St. Petersburg. When my old man died, I held up the funeral for three days, thinking they would come. But they didn't come. I suppose they never got my telegram Then, when the war began, all my sons were taken as soldiers. And no matter how many times I wrote and inquired, they could tell me nothing about them. Just like a stone thrown in the water."

"Perhaps they are prisoners ?"

" No ; I think they are gone."

Again the grandmother remembered something bitter ; again spoke in her good voice :

" And when the *children* came, they set fire to my little house, and left only the ashes. I wept, and I said to them : ' Oh, don't set it on fire—do let it alone ! ' ' So you want to live with the Germans ! You're a German woman ! We'll throw you into the fire ! ' I thought to myself : Let them throw me in ; as it is, mine is a hard life, and all of God's saints have been burnt. I stand there and think to myself, and they are arguing. One says : ' Let's throw her into the fire ! ' And the other says : ' No, let her alone ! ' Then, when the house burnt down, I went away. It took me three months, going on foot."

The grandmother became lost in thought. Was she thinking of her house—there at the end of the world, where charred bits of wood alone remained under the snow ? Or was she thinking of her sons, who had worked in the factory here, and were now out there—there under the snow ?

And I thought, as I looked at the bowed grandmother, who had grown silent (the whole car was now looking at her) :

" Grandmother, you with your heart, which has suffered bitter loss ; with your white heart you have accepted your bitter fate—otherwise how could you speak of your despoilers as your *children* ?—and now you are alone in the white world with your white heart, and your life is hard ; you are living your last days, and who is there to comfort you ? Who will comfort us ? Grandmother, it is hard for us too ; I speak for all, and to all, all, all. Who feels at ease, who can feel happy at the sight of the white ruins of your house, at the sight of the white grave of your lost world ? What wild beast, or what leering, shaggy soul ; or what soul, crushed, like a rotten, worm-eaten mushroom, or heart resembling a gnawed dry bone ? No ; here we are, all of us ; and if there is anyone who has not understood with his mind, then he has felt it with his heart—every one of us—your oppressive burden . . . the whole cross is ours to bear !"

"Don't be uneasy," said the grandmother. "A woman in Moscow had a dream. She dreamt of Virgin Mary, who said to her : ' The Russian kingdom is in my hand ; go and seek such an ikon as will show me as I am now.' That same woman went all over Moscow, through all the churches and into all the houses—and she couldn't find it. At last she went to the village of Kolomensk, near Moscow, and went into a church that had been built in the times of Ivan the Terrible. It was full of ikons—they were lying there below, one on top the other, like slabs of the dead. She picked up one after the

other, one after the other, and suddenly exclaimed :
' That's the very one ! ' And now this ikon is
being taken all over Moscow, and prayers are
being offered it for salvation. And I saw it.
At the top a kind of rainbow and Sabaoth, then
clouds, and then Virgin Mary in porphyry and
crown—in one hand the sceptre, in the other the
earth."

It was now time for the grandmother to leave
the tram.

We left together ; it was easy for us to leave,
for every one made way for us.

I led the old grandmother to a stopping-place,
saw her into another tram, and said good-bye.

" Good-bye, grandmother ! "

" Christ be with you ! "

And I went my way, through the St. Petersburg
darkness, and in the darkness bore along with
me in a white heart—a tranquil light.

The Betrothed

THE BETROTHED

THREE years a lad played with a lass, three autumns. Countless were the words spoken in whispers. That was how Maria loved Ivan !

Who among us, nowadays, loves like that ?

The time came to put blossoms in the hair. And Maria was given to another ; she was not given to Ivan.

Quickly the parents made the match between them. A nice, well-to-do son-in-law was found ; the old folk were pleased with themselves.

And there was no more honey in life for her ; dark grew the face of Maria, even darker than an autumnal night. Only her eyes flickered, flickered like two candles.

Her soul was weary, a frosty cold congealed her heart. Desolate, she sang in the evening her dolorous songs. Death itself would have been welcomer. Yet bravely she resigned herself, and bravely endured.

Three years Maria lived with the ungracious one, three autumns. And one day she fell ill. She did not pine a long time, but died during the feast of Kusma and Demian.

And they buried Maria.

O ho ! the winter had come, with its frosts ; white snow covered the grave ! And Maria lay under the white snow ; no longer flickered those eyes, the eyelids were sealed over them.

One night Maria rose from her grave ; she went to her husband.

A sign of the cross made he, Feodor her husband, the ungracious one.

" What does she want, the accursed one ? " and he would not let his wife in.

Maria then went to her father, to her mother she went.

" At whom are you gaping ? " said her father.

" Where, witch, are you going ? " said her mother.

The father was frightened, the mother was frightened ; they would not let their daughter into the house.

Maria went to her godmother.

" Get you away, soul of a sinner, where you will, there is no room for you here," and away sent the godmother her godchild.

And Maria was now left alone, a stranger in this wide world ; no other roof had she than the sky.

" I will go to him, to my first one, my earlier one," thought Maria suddenly. " He will take me in ! "

And she appeared before Ivan's window.

Near the window she could see Ivan sitting ; he was painting a picture of the Virgin Mary.

She knocked on the window.

Then Ivan wakened his servant. It was

night, and together they went out with hatchets.

The servant, when he saw Maria, was frightened. Without looking round once, he ran away.

She looked at Ivan.

"Take me in. I will not harm you."

Ivan was overjoyed ; he approached her, and he embraced her.

"Stop !" she cried. "Don't press me so tightly ; my bones have lain idle for some time."

And she herself kept looking at him, she could not tear her eyes away ; she caressed him, and could not caress him enough. That was how Maria loved Ivan !

Who among us, nowadays, loves like that ?

Ivan took Maria into his house. He did not show her to anyone ; he gave her dresses, also food and drink. And thus they lived until Christmas together.

On Christmas Day they went to church. In the church all began to look at Maria—her father and her mother, her husband Feodor and her godmother.

When the service ended Maria went over to her mother.

"Yes, I am your own," said Maria. "You will remember that one night I came to you, and none of you would let me in, and so I went to my first one, my earlier one, and he took me in."

THE CLOCK

And they all acknowledged Maria, and they gave judgment ; they gave her not to her old husband Feodor, but they gave her to Ivan.

O ho ! the spring had come, the snows had thawed away, the green grass sprang up, and upon the little Red Hill were wedded Ivan and Maria.

Here is an end to my tale, an end to my novel.

Easter

EASTER

GREAT was the dark of night and great the sadness that spread on Easter Eve across the Russian land, from the Volga to the sea, from the sea to the mountains.

The sad night was lost in the sad stillness—there was no sound nor glimmer of light.

The old bell-ringer climbed to the belfry. The old bell-ringer would sound the large Easter bell.

"Why such gloom and sadness across the whole Russian land?"

"There is gloom and sadness across the Russian land. . . . It is the souls of the sinners and of the cut-throats, rising from the depths, from the darkness, from the abysses, from across the river of fire, from the blackest of gaols—swarming in a respite to their radiant native land, to rest from agonizing torments, to find a drop of dew wherewith to wet their lips. The native dead rise up from the native fields—there is my mother, there are my brothers and my sisters. I also see : there are many of them, the weary and the forsaken ; the down-trodden, and those without shelter ; whole hosts of these are coming to greet their kin. I see also a pilgrim ; he is dressed in white, and there is a cross in his hand. . . ."

And the gloom and the sadness dim one's eyes.

THE CLOCK

Midnight was near.

The people raised up the sacred banners, they lit the red candles, they carried out in procession the ikons of the altar.

And the bell-ringer sounded the resonant bell.

The resonant bell rang, and the darkness turned into a whirlwind and dispersed itself.

The souls of the sinners and of the cut-throats began to sob, their blood-red tears became white. The dead scattered through the street—they kissed their dear ones, those whom they love ; they exchanged the Easter kiss with the living, just as the living do.

And the Holy Mother, the Three-day Resurrection, having washed herself with spring dew, set alight the dawn, and, after Mass had been said, she led her all adorned upon a high mountain.

And the dawn spread out from the East to the West, from the Volga to the sea, from the sea to the mountains.

And a life-giving cross arose in the dawn.

The cross of resurrection flamed in the sun across the Russian land ; it flamed in the dawn at sunrise, and until broad daylight.

And he who awaited Him saw the cross.

Glory be to Thee, Blessed Sun, glory to Thee.